The New Millennium Girls

Isabel's Secret

by

Jan May

New Millennium Girl Books

New Millennium Girl Books
690 Laurel Drive
Aurora, Il 60506
www.NewMillenniumGirlBooks.com
Printed in the United States of America
By New Millennium Girl Books
ISBN 978-0-9835281-0-4

Third Edition

Cover by Julianna Davis
Graphics by Vince Corcoran

For Rachel,
my beloved daughter and
inspiration

Contents

Chapter One
The Secret

Holly held up her watch. "Get ready, Izzy… Get set… Go!"

Isabel tightened her red bandana and took five steps backward. Then she darted forward, grabbed a fistful of Starlight's mane, and flung herself onto the horse's back. Her heart jumped. She gave him a kick. "Hee-yah!"

Starlight whinnied and tossed his head into the morning air, then bolted across the field like he was being chased by wild bees.

Holly jumped up and down. "You're going to do it, Izzy!" she shouted. "You'll be Misty Springs' winner again!"

The chilly November air swished Isabel's black hair across her face. Her knees gripped Starlight's sides. Together they raced past the tree house she and Holly had built five summers ago. They galloped past the pumpkin patch she and Mom planted this spring. They sprinted past the tree-lined slopes and into the wide-open rangeland of the Angel Ridge Ranch.

"Winners never quit," she chanted, "and quitters never win, because I serve the mighty God that lives deep within!"

Isabel Morningsky never did anything halfway. It was November, but sweat beaded her forehead and dripped into her dark-brown eyes. She swiped away the drops and leaned forward. Small rocks shot up from under Starlight's hooves. Isabel could feel the rumbling of his gait on the dirt as they rounded the oak tree.

"Get up!" she shouted. A cloud of dust rose from the ground and covered her boots. "Come on, boy!" She nudged harder with her foot. "You can do it! We'll take back the gold cup from Kip Johnson. That'll show him. Don't tell me a girl can't race as fast as a boy!"

Starlight snorted as if he understood every word and picked up the pace all the way back to the ranch.

Holly stood on the corral fence with her wavy blonde hair pulled back by a lavender headband that matched her shorts. She raised her arm like a flag then lowered it as Isabel and Starlight flashed by.

"Ladies and gentlemen," said Holly, pretending to be an announcer. "Eleven-year-old, soon-to-be-twelve, Is-a-bel Morn-ing-sky, Misty Spring, Colorado's new winner of the bareback competition!"

Isabel pulled back hard on the reins, and Starlight skidded to a halt. Isabel jumped down and trotted over to Holly, panting. "How fast was I?"

"Six minutes, forty seconds. You beat your time!"

Isabel slapped her leg. "Rats! I still need twenty more seconds to beat Kip Johnson. She frowned and looked down. "Losing two years in a row is such a disgrace. Besides," she said, glancing up at Holly, "I hate the way he gloats when he wins."

"Everyone does," said Holly, folding her arms.

Isabel's heart sank as she petted Starlight's nose. "I know you did your best." She grabbed his reins and tugged. "Come on, Holly, let's give Starlight a drink."

That night Isabel lay wide-eyed in her bed, staring out her window at the starry night sky. The annual Thanksgiving Day Bareback Race was only three days away. She *had* to win the title back from

Kip Johnson this year or she would never live it down. Kip had moved from Kentucky two years ago, where he'd been a champion in jumping competitions. She had to admit, he was a pretty sharp rider, but so stuck up!

Isabel rolled over and tapped her fingers on the nightstand. *And the way he brags about boys being better riders than girls!* Isabel punched her pillow. Then she jumped out of bed and paced back and forth. "How can I make Starlight run faster?" she murmured.

Little shivers of joy filled Isabel's heart at the thought of Starlight. The moonlight had shone through the barn window the crisp October night he was born. It lit up the white star on his little brown head. Isabel knew instantly his name should be Starlight. Once he could stand up, she'd stroked his soft mane. He looked at her with big brown eyes and nuzzled her.

Isabel sighed at the memory. It was one of the best nights of her life. *Kindred spirits,* she thought, *right from the start. Maybe I should go out to the barn and check on him right now.*

Isabel pulled on her jeans, tucked in her nightgown, and crept down the hall. When she reached the top of the stairs, a voice startled her from the downstairs den. There was no mistaking her Grandmother Biltmore's sharp tone.

"Isabel is a complete mess. She doesn't comb her hair, and she smells like a swamp. For goodness' sake, she is almost twelve years old!"

Isabel looked in the hall mirror. "Geesh!" she whispered, flattening her hair with her hands. "It's not *that* bad."

Isabel knew Gran could be difficult. Like the time Isabel wanted to bake Mom's special cookies for their tea party last summer. Grandmother Biltmore had insisted they drive into town and purchase two dozen pink and white petit fours from Camilla's Bakery instead. Isabel had no idea what a petit four was, but Grandmother Biltmore insisted that she *should* know. Isabel licked her lips at the thought. She did love those sweet, tiny, iced squared cakes with crème inside. That's when Grandmother Biltmore asked Isabel to call her Gran.

*Hmmm…*Isabel thought. *Things always seem to work out. Maybe Gran's ranting this time is just like one of those other times.*

Isabel could hear her mom pipe in, "Now, Mother, I know Isabel may not be the perfect little lady, but she is amazingly smart. Do you know that she knows almost as much about horses as any rancher around here does? She raised Starlight from a foal and trained him all by herself."

That's it. You tell her, Mom, thought Isabel, pursing her lips. She crept down the stairs further to peek into the room.

"This ranch!" said Gran, throwing up her hands. "I was hoping it would be financial security for Isabel's future. She looks and smells more like a ranch *hand.*"

Mom's face turned red, like she might explode any minute. Isabel held her breath to hear what she would say.

"She's happy and healthy," Mom said. "That's what matters."

Isabel grinned and nodded. Happy and healthy for sure! How could Gran not love the flower-covered hills that perched outside her front door? They were Isabel's best friend. Or the horses! Isabel shivered with delight thinking about them. It was magical riding on the back of a horse, anytime you wanted. She felt so free on Angel Ridge Ranch. It was so much a part of her. She could never leave it.

Isabel could hear Gran's voice like a whistling tea kettle boiling over with hot steam. She leaned closer.

"Next year she'll be a teenager," Gran huffed. "You can't stop her from growing up, Grace. Who is she really going to meet out here? In Boston she could meet young men from all the finest families. Someone who could" — Gran hesitated — "give her a future."

Mom scowled. "You mean . . . unlike Isabel's father?"

"Hmph," Gran grunted.

Isabel knew Gran didn't approve of Dad. She always talked "down" to him, sniffed, and put her nose in the air whenever Dad was in the room. Isabel's blood boiled just thinking about it.

She glanced up at the family pictures on the wall. Dad was a wild, dark-haired, modern-day cowboy when Mom met him at a rodeo that day. Dad always told her it was love at first sight.

Isabel peeked back in the room.

Mom stood up and paced over near the window. "People who are born with money are no better than those who get it through honest work."

Grandmother Biltmore sat tall in her chair and straightened her white nightdress. "I've come to a decision. I've decided to take back the loan I gave you for the ranch."

Isabel ducked back on the stairs and clapped a hand over her mouth to keep her gasp inside. *No ranch?*

Mom's voice was quivering. "What? Mother, you can't do that. It would kill Sam. He's put his heart and soul into this ranch. If you would take just five minutes of your time to look around, you'd see what a great job he's done with it."

"You mean raising smelly sheep and horses?"

Isabel could see her mother's shadow pacing back and forth.

"You're impossible!" said Mom.

"All right," said Gran. "Keep the ranch, but Isabel comes to Boston with me to attend a private school for girls. Maybe we can somehow stop this runaway train."

Isabel couldn't believe her ears. *Tear me away from the ranch and haul me back to Boston? No!* Isabel shook her head. "Of all the mean things to do, Gran," she whispered. "I thought we were friends."

"This is not the Old West, Mother," Mom said. "It's the twenty-first century. Woman can be anything they want to be." She raised her voice. "You're never happy unless you're controlling someone's life, are you, Mother? It's the Biltmore way, after all. Well, you're not going to control Isabel's."

"She's going to find out the truth soon enough, Grace. She's getting older. Then where will her future be?"

Mom sighed. "I wish we'd never kept it a secret. I knew it was a mistake from the beginning. Now you're trying to use it against us."

Isabel sat on the stairs with her head in her hands. Grandmother Biltmore's words pierced her heart like a dagger. *What secret? Why did they keep it from me? I can't leave Misty Springs and go to Boston. I just can't!*

Isabel sprang to her feet. *I won't!* She carefully crept down the stairs, sneaking past the den, and fled outside into the cold night air. She marched across the yard as if she were going to war. She clenched her teeth and slapped her fist in her hand. "Why would Gran do this? I don't understand!"

Isabel whistled low when she walked into the barn. Starlight walked over to the stall door. His soft lips nipped at her pockets, looking for a treat. Isabel reached out and stroked his soft neck. "Sorry, boy," she said. "I didn't have time to get one." She tilted her head and thought for a moment. "What did Gran mean about taking back the loan on the ranch? What loan?"

Isabel couldn't imagine life without Angel Ridge Ranch. She loved waking up before the sun every morning and hearing the last cricket sing at night. She didn't mind the hard work of feeding the horses or mucking out the stalls. It all felt so right.

"Starlight, I don't understand. Will Mom and Dad lose the ranch if I don't go to Gran's snooty old school?"

Isabel slid down on a pile of hay like a limp noodle and stared at the wooden ceiling. "What are we going to do?" She lay there for a good long time, chewing on a piece of hay and trying to figure out how to stop Grandmother Biltmore's terrible plan.

Isabel yawned. She was too weary to keep on worrying. She cuddled up on the hay. "Winners never quit," she mumbled, "and quitters never..."

Isabel slipped off into a restless sleep before she could finish the sentence.

Chapter Two
Makeover Magic

Early in the morning the rooster crowed, waking
Isabel. She stretched and sat up with her hair full of
straw and blinked at Starlight. He nudged her with
his nose and looked down at her, then whinnied
softly. She ran her hand over his cheeks and ears.
"Hey, boy."

Isabel rubbed the sleep from her eyes and looked
around. *Why was she in the barn?* The thoughts of last
night's conversation with Mom and Gran flooded
back to her. She bit her lip. What was she going to
do? She stood to her feet and paced back and forth.

All of a sudden an idea popped into her head. "I
know! If I can prove that I am becoming a young

lady right here in Misty Springs, maybe Grandmother Biltmore won't make such a fuss. Mom and Gran won't have to be mad at each other. Then I won't have to go to Boston, and Dad can keep the ranch."

Isabel swiped her hands back and forth like she had just finished a job. "It's as easy as that!" Isabel hugged Starlight's neck and kissed his nose. "It's perfect! Starlight, you're the best listener ever!"

Isabel dashed out of the barn, across the yard, and into the house. She flew up to her bedroom, closing and locking the door behind her. Diving on the bed, she reached for her cell phone.

"Holly," she texted, "I want you to come over and give me a" — she could hardly text the last line — "a makeover."

"No way! YK," Holly texted back. "You hate girly things. Is this a joke?"

"I'll tell you when you get here, just hurry."

Isabel nervously dropped the phone, dove under the covers, and clutched her pillow. "I sure hope this works," she croaked.

Twenty minutes later, Holly arrived at Isabel's bedroom door and peeked into her room. "Knock, knock! Team Blonde at your service." Holly waltzed into Isabel's room, toting a pink, polka-dotted bag brimming with beauty products.

Isabel sat on the bed with her knees pulled up to her chest, feeling sheepish. "Thanks for coming."

"What's going on?"

"I overheard my grandmother talking to my mom last night. She sounded so mad! She wants me to go to some school in Boston that will make me more *ladylike*."

Holly's eyes grew wide and she plopped down on the bed next to Isabel. "You? Ladylike? The world's most dedicated tomboy? Whoa! That's bad."

"I thought if you could help me to be more ladylike, maybe she would stop pressuring my parents to make me go with her to Boston."

"I have just the thing. I'll give you the full Holly Haddleburg treatment." Holly put her hands on her hips. "First," she said, "Let's take a look at that hair." She motioned to Isabel. "Go on, take the hat off."

Isabel slowly reached up and took off her Colorado Rockies baseball cap.

Holly stepped back and gasped. "Yikes! You've got big problems." She reached into her bag and pulled out two bottles of lavender shampoo and conditioner. "Uh huh. These ought to do the trick."

Isabel grimaced and closed her eyes. She hated those girly-smelling shampoos.

"Come on," coaxed Holly, taking Isabel by the hand. "Down to the bathroom." Holly reached into her pocket and pulled out two tootsie pops. "But first, something sweet to take away the sting."

"It's like the last supper," said Isabel grimly. "I'll take the grape."

Soon, Isabel was leaning over the sink with soapy hair. Holly massaged in essence of lavender shampoo. "I know," she said, "Let's bake something really scrumptious for your Thanksgiving dinner — something your grandmother will never forget." She slurped on her sucker and scrubbed harder.

Isabel blinked shampoo out of her eyes. "Your chocolatly-caramel fudge that won the blue ribbon at the fair last year?"

"Mmm," said Holly, "you mean the chocolaty wonder? Okay, but I can't give you the recipe. It's a secret."

Isabel wrapped a towel around her hair and sat on the edge of the bath tub. She smiled with her purple lips. "You're the best friend ever."

Holly's blue eyes twinkled. "That's my job!"

Isabel couldn't believe how long it took to gel, blow-dry, spray, and flatten her hair. It was no wonder why she never took the time to mess with it. She would be old and gray before she ever finished.

Holly took a deep breath and stepped back to admire her work. "I love the way it looks straightened, Izzy," she squealed. "I've been dying to do this for months!" Holly reached out to grab Isabel's hand. "Time for your nails."

Isabel moaned and hid her hands behind her back. "Not the nails!"

Holly put her hands on her hips. "Come on, Izzy. You want this to work, don't you?"

Isabel slowly held her hands out in front of her.

Holly inspected them like she was a doctor. "Hmmm. Uh huh. Oh dear. Do you even use soap on them? These will need some cuticle cream, filing, and soaking. And I'll show you how the lady at Team Blonde in town massages your hands. It's simply heav-en-ly!" She gave Isabel a little push. "Sit back, relax, and let your cares float away on the waves of lavender fragrance."

Isabel frowned.

Holly chuckled. "Honestly, Izzy, you're gonna love it."

Isabel leaned back in the chair and closed her eyes tight. She doubted she would love it. In fact, she already hated it.

Holly carefully applied the pink glittery polish to each finger. *Why does it have to be pink? And glittery,* thought Isabel, *the two things I hate the most?* Isabel inhaled the fumes and coughed. *I'm going to die. I know the smell of this nail polish alone is going to kill me.* She covered her nose. *They'll have to bury me under the old oak tree. With my boots on, of course.*

"Now, open your fingers to let them dry," instructed Holly. "Don't touch *anything* while I have a look around." She pranced over to Isabel's closet and inspected her clothing like she was a fashion designer. "Nope," she said, throwing the Colorado Rockies' t-shirt on the bed. "Nope, too short," she said, sliding the pants down the closet rod. "Oh dear, no, too baggie! Next, too bright. Next, too dull. I always thought you had some really cute clothes, Izzy. Where did you hide them?"

"Maybe I got rid of those." She didn't want Holly to find the *really cute girly clothes*. Her heart beat faster and she squirmed. *Don't look in the back of the closet, Holly.* She held her breath.

"What is this?" Holly asked, "hiding way in the back?" She tugged hard and pulled the garment loose.

"Ugh," moaned Isabel.

Holly beamed and held up a blue chiffon dress with a lace collar like she'd just won the grand prize at the fair. "It's perfect, Izzy!"

"It was my birthday present from Gran last year," Isabel said, scowling. She wrinkled her nose. "It's hideous!"

Holly raised an eyebrow.

Uh oh, thought Isabel. "No. No way. You know I hate dresses."

A sneaky grin spilled across Holly's face. "Izzy, Izzy, Izzy. *This* is our secret weapon!"

❖

The next day, Mom and Grandmother Biltmore drove into town to shop. As soon as the car disappeared down the long, tree-lined driveway, Isabel and Holly went to work making Holly's blue-ribbon, chocolaty-caramel fudge.

"You dump in the chocolate chips," said Holly, "and stir until it melts."

"All right." Isabel opened the bag of chocolate chips. "Maybe I need to taste these first, to make sure they're all right," she giggled.

"Me too," said Holly, smiling. She held out her hand.

"Mmm, yep, there're good!" Isabel poured the bag into the pan.

"Now, I'll add the sugar and milk," said Holly. She measured out one cup of each and added it to the chocolate chips.

Isabel barely breathed while she held the pan steady, like the concoction might explode if she let go. *I could never cook as well as Holly or Mom.*

"There," said Holly, stirring it together. "Now it just has to cook."

Isabel let out a sigh of relief. *This looks easy enough.* She really wanted to impress Gran.

Holly stirred the sweet mixture one more time and turned the burner on low. Then she smiled at Isabel. "Let's crank up the radio while the chocolate chips melt."

Giggling, the girls held their spoons like microphones to sing along as they danced around the kitchen. Isabel grabbed the broom and twirled it around like it was her partner. "Oops!" She accidentally knocked a bag of potato chips off the counter, spilling them onto the floor.

"Don't worry, I'll pick these up," said Holly, bending down. "You check on the chocolate."

Isabel inspected the chocolate on the stove. "Hmmm." It wasn't melting yet. *I'll just turn it up a bit. Maybe a lot.* She reached over and turned it up two notches.

The girls started singing again and pretended they were in a band. "Watch, Holly," said Isabel, strumming the broom like a guitar.

All of a sudden, Holly stopped and wrinkled her nose. "What's that funny smell?" She hurried over to the stove and bent over the pan. She gasped. "Ew! Izzy, this smells awful! The chocolate is scorched. What did you do?"

Isabel bit her lip. *Why, oh, why, didn't I pay attention?*

Holly looked like she was going to faint. Isabel picked up a magazine from the table and fanned Holly with it. "Don't worry, Holly, it'll be okay. You'll see," said Isabel, hoping.

"But it was the grand-prize winner." Holly plopped down on the kitchen chair. "You killed it!"

She shook her head and moaned. "What are we going to do now?"

Isabel didn't want to say it, but it was the last resort. "I guess we'll have to rely on the secret weapon."

Holly rolled her eyes. "Please, God, help us!"

When Thanksgiving morning arrived, Isabel swished down the stairs in the "secret weapon" — her blue chiffon dress. *It doesn't feel elegant,* thought Isabel, trying not to scratch. But she wanted to make an impression on Gran. Isabel's hair was combed, pinned in place, and tied with a blue satin ribbon. She felt like if she moved the wrong way everything would fall apart.

Isabel heard the thumping of Dad's cowboy boots on the floor as he walked out of the kitchen. He stood at the bottom of the stairs and grinned. "Grace, come in here," he said. "You have to see this."

Mom dashed in from the kitchen, wiping her hands on her apron, and stood with her mouth wide open. "Isabel Maya Morningsky, is that you?" She put her hand up to her cheek in awe. "And with high-heel shoes?"

"Yep. It's me. Do you like it?" Isabel twirled around. Then . . . "Yikes!" Isabel's foot missed the step as she twirled. "Oh no!"she cried, trying to catch her balance. "Come on, Izzy," she mumbled. "Winners never quit."

But the heel of her other shoe caught on a scarf she'd left lying on the stairs yesterday. With a shriek, she tumbled down the last few steps.

Thud! Isabel landed at her parents' feet in a puffy blue chiffon heap.

Dad reached out to grab her. "Isabel!"

"Are you okay?" asked Mom, hovering over her.

Grandmother Biltmore poked her head around the corner. "What's all the fuss about?"

Perfect timing, Gran.

Isabel's hair was a shambles. It fell over her brown eyes in wild hanks. Her dress lay draped around her, wrinkled and sloppy, with a tear across the bottom.

Gran smirked. "What did I tell you? It's disgraceful they way Isabel has become a wild girl."

Isabel's face turned three shades of red. She couldn't look Gran in the eye.

"Izzy just tripped, that's all," Dad said, helping her up.

Isabel held back tears. *Lord,* she thought, *I think I need another secret weapon.*

Mom helped Isabel straighten her dress. "The tear isn't too bad, honey," she comforted. "We'll fix it after dinner." Isabel felt like her balloon of hope had been popped. *How am I ever going to save the ranch now?*

Dad took Isabel by the arm and escorted her to the dinner table as if she were a grand lady, despite her disheveled appearance. Isabel sat down and slumped over. A tear welled up in the corner of one eye, but she quickly brushed it aside. Her heels pinched her feet, and her dress itched. *Winners never quit,* she recited in her mind, *and quitters never win, for I serve the mighty God that lives deep within.*

The comfort of those words and the smell of hot, buttery mashed potatoes encouraged her and she sat up. *Gran might be able to beat me,* thought Isabel, *but she'll never beat God.*

After Dad said the blessing, Isabel dipped her fork into the creamy whipped potatoes on her plate.

"I've been thinking, Isabel," said Grandmother Biltmore coyly. "How would you like to spend a year with me in Boston?"

Isabel's fork stopped halfway to her mouth. *Oh, please don't ruin my Thanksgiving dinner with this kind of talk!* She looked at Dad with pleading eyes.

Dad gaped at Mom as if he'd just been jolted by lightning.

Grandmother Biltmore tossed her head. "Boston is beautiful in the fall. You could make a lot of nice friends and maybe go to riding school," she coaxed.

Dad turned to Gran. "Gertrude, Isabel already knows how to ride, and quite well, thank you."

Isabel's heart thumped. She didn't like the angry look on her dad's face. *Now that my secret weapon failed, Gran will certainly take our ranch if I say no.* Isabel chewed on her lip. *Quitters never win and winners never quit...* She took a deep breath and stood up. "Yes!" she blurted. "Yes, Gran, I'd like to ..." Isabel lost her nerve, "to *think* about going to Boston."

Gran looked at Dad with a sly smile. "Wonderful. But don't think too long, dear. Arrangements must be made soon."

Isabel slunk down in her chair. *Why did I say I would think about it?*

The rest of Thanksgiving dinner lost all its charm. Even the pumpkin pie lost its flavor, and it was her favorite.

Isabel and Dad sat quietly. But Grandmother Biltmore was all smiles, like she had just won a grand prize. She yakked away with Mom about her new neighbors, the Pickadillys, and where on earth did they get such a disgraceful last name? And one must always have the latest styles in clothing so you could be presentable in all the social gatherings.

Mom sighed and rolled her eyes.

Would Gran ever change and talk about something worthwhile? Isabel wondered.

Finally, Gran excused herself and scuttled up to the guest room to pack her things.

"Isabel, are you sure this is what you want?" Mom asked when Gran had left the table.

Isabel looked down. *I must be brave to save the ranch.* "It might be fun. For sure it would be different. I've" — her voice choked on her words — "I've never been to Boston."

Dad's eyes blazed like fire as he stood up. "This is all nonsense. It's time for the race, Izzy. Go upstairs and get ready."

Isabel gulped. In her misery over Grandmother Biltmore, she had forgotten about the race. She kicked off her heels and rushed upstairs to change. She could hear Dad's boots stomping around the kitchen; his loud, irritated voice filled the house. A few seconds later, the back door slammed shut with a crash.

Isabel didn't know what to do. She peeked out of her room. Mom was carrying Gran's suitcase down the hall. Isabel sat in the hall, slumped over to the floor, and leaned her head in her hands. This was the biggest problem she'd ever had to face.

"Think about what I said, Grace. I'd like an answer by the spring term," said Gran.

Mom nodded quietly.

Why does it feel like a thunder storm every time Grandmother Biltmore visits? thought Isabel. "This is terrible. This is horrible. This is catastrophic! What am I going to do?"

Dad's piercing voice broke into Isabel's trance. "Iz-zy! It's time to go! Get a move on!"

Isabel pulled herself up and hurried to her room to grab her cowboy hat. She plopped it on and trotted down the stairs. *I can't worry about this now,* she thought, *I have a race to win!*

Chapter Three
The Race

Isabel leaned her head against the back seat of the pickup truck as they drove to the race. She didn't feel very well. Too many things were swirling around her head. *I have to stop Gran and I have to beat Kip Johnson."*

Isabel tried counting appaloosas as they drove; that always made her feel better. But not today. It was as if a giant, dark cloud had enveloped her and was trying to suffocate her.

Starlight whinnied when they arrived at the fairgrounds. They drove under a huge orange banner draped across the road. The banner displayed a turkey and the words: **Misty Springs 25th Annual Thanksgiving Day Bareback Race**.

Dad brought the truck to a stop next to the red animal barn. Isabel rolled down the window and leaned out to see Kip Johnson warming up his stallion, Boss, around the race track. The horse's midnight-black coat shimmered in the afternoon sun.

Isabel sighed. "He's beautiful, Dad, and he runs like lightning." She wrinkled her forehead. "He might beat Starlight."

"Starlight has spirit, Izzy." Dad said, "and you've been riding him hard for weeks now. He's ready."

Isabel fidgeted. "You're probably right." But deep down inside she wasn't sure. She hopped out of the truck and backed Starlight out of the trailer. When Boss rounded the corner of the track near her, Starlight snorted and stomped the ground.

"Look at him, Izzy," Dad said, grinning. "I think he wants to beat that stallion as bad as you do."

Isabel felt better knowing Starlight wanted to win, too. She felt electricity bubble up her arms. The color returned to her cheeks. She wanted to beat Kip Johnson more than anything. More than catching the huge bullfrog in the creek that kept hopping out of her grasp. More than getting that fancy new saddle for Christmas. More than not going to Boston . . .

She hesitated. *Well, almost more than anything.*

The crowd began to gather in the bleachers, carrying plaid blankets and thermoses filled with warm drinks. The smell of cinnamon apple cider and caramel popcorn wafted from the food stands. Isabel inhaled. "Mmmm! It always smells so good here. Look Mom, there's Mrs. Paddington."

"Isn't she a good neighbor?" asked Mom.

Isabel nodded. "I bet she brought her famous apple and pumpkin pies to sell." Her stomach rumbled at the thought.

Dad smiled. "No time to think about food now, Izzy. It's time to warm up Starlight."

Boss rounded the curve near them. Kip shot her a defiant glance. Her heart dropped down to her stomach.

"Whoa," Kip said, slowing down in front of her. He narrowed his beady green eyes and smirked. "Yep," he said, patting Boss, "I got myself a real champion here."

"Starlight's fast too," she blurted out.

"Yeah, but it's too bad he has a girl riding him." He kicked Boss, "Get up!"

Why does he have to brag all the time? Isabel felt like someone punched her in the gut. *You'll find out who can ride. Just wait and see!* Isabel took a deep breath and paced up and down. *I can do this.*

Starlight stomped his foot.

She looked at Dad.

"Don't let this kid throw you, Izzy. He's trying to psyche you out. You got this. Stay focused," said Dad.

Mom smiled. "We're rooting for you."

"Okay, here I go." Isabel gulped and mounted Starlight. She settled herself onto his broad, bare back and trotted him out to the track along the rest of the contestants. *I can do this!* "Winners never quit," she whispered under her breath, "and quitters never win."

Observing the other riders, Isabel had to admit there were some fast horses out there. Tyler Thomas's paint horse, Scout, came in second three years ago. *But he was always nice about winning.* Chloe Davis had been racing her chestnut mare, Sandy, at the local rodeos. She could rope a calf too. *I better watch out for her,* thought Isabel.

Isabel's palms were sweaty. She didn't mind if the others won. The only one she really wanted to beat was Kip Johnson.

The announcer's voice came over the loudspeakers. "Riders, it's time to begin the race. Lead your horses behind the starting line."

Isabel hopped down and took hold of Starlight's bridle. Kip Johnson dismounted Boss. He glanced over at Isabel and sneered. His green hat matched his eyes. With his pug nose, Isabel thought he looked like a leprechaun.

She chuckled to herself at the thought, *Why am so I worried about this kid?* Isabel acknowledged his taunt and glared back. "May the best person win," she said.

The sight of all the horses with their riders sent a tingle of excitement up Isabel's spine. She loved a good race.

The announcer raised his gun. "On your mark . . Get set . . . Go!" A loud shot burst into the air. All sixteen contestants rushed over to their horses, grabbed their manes, and leaped onto their backs.

Tyler Thomas's horse, Scout, spooked, backed up, and knocked Isabel down.

"Sorry," he said, looking down at her.

"Go, Izzy, go!" shouted Dad from the sideline.

"Is this too rough for girls?" chided Kip, jumping up and mounting Boss.

Isabel gritted her teeth and shot to her feet like a rocket. "We'll see about that!"

Isabel took five steps back and ran with all her might. She grabbed Starlight's mane, flung herself onto his back, and gave him a firm squeeze. "Hee yah!"

Starlight took off with a jolt and galloped like a flash behind the group of riders. The dust from the horses' hooves rose and stung Isabel eyes. "Grrr!" She closed her eyes and wiped them on her sleeve. "Winners never quit," she chanted, "and quitters never win, for I serve the mighty God that lives deep within!"

Isabel dug her heels in. She yelled over the rumbling of the horses' hooves, "Fly, Starlight, fly!"

Starlight's ears pricked up, and he snorted like a wild stallion. He caught up with Tyler Thomas and Scout. They galloped together in a pack as they rounded the first checkpoint.

Isabel passed Chloe and Sandy. She quickly glanced over her shoulder and saw four other riders close on her heels.

Isabel's heart hammered in her chest. She could see Kip and Boss only two horses ahead.

Kip turned around and shot a dagger at her with his eyes. She glared at him. *What do you think now, Kentucky boy?* "Hee-yah!" she yelled.

Kip crouched even lower over Boss and shouted, "Go! Go, hee-*yah!*

The sound of pounding hooves rang in Isabel's ears as she pushed Starlight harder. The wind whipped her jet-black hair into her face. She bent down and whispered, "You're a champion, Starlight, whether you win or not. But today, let's win."

Starlight was only a head behind Boss as they rounded the second checkpoint.

"Give it all ya got, Starlight!" Starlight lunged forward. Now, Boss and Starlight were neck in neck as they headed for the finish line.

The fans rose to their feet and cheered wildly. Starlight was sweaty, and Isabel felt like she was going to slip off. She grabbed onto his mane tighter. "Just a little more, boy," she urged.

Suddenly, a cloud of dust rose up and hid them as they crossed the finish line. Isabel could hear voices.

"Who won?" asked Dad, running over to the race track.

"It must be a photo finish," said Mom. "We'll have to wait for the judges to tell us."

Minutes seemed like hours as Isabel paced back and forth, waiting for the decision. This was worse than waiting for Christmas. She looked over at Kip. He stuck his nose in the air and straightened his vest.

"The decision is in, folks," stated the announcer. "Will the contestants who finished first, Isabel Morningsky and Kip Johnson, please come to the podium? It hasn't happened in a long time," he said, "but it looks like we have a tie for first place."

"Yahoo!" shouted Isabel. She gave Starlight a big hug. "I knew you could do it!"

"Izzy, I'm so proud of you!" Isabel ran into her dad's arms. He squeezed her tight. "Your hard work paid off."

Isabel breathed a sigh of relief. "Thanks, Dad. I wasn't so sure with Kip trying to psyche me out."

"You were awesome, honey," said Mom, kissing her cheek.

Isabel glowed when the judge slipped a shiny gold medal around her neck. It hung from a beautiful, blue ribbon. She didn't even mind tying with Kip.

But Kip Johnson's face looked like he had just sucked on a sour pickle. "It's not fair," he grunted when he received his medal. Isabel couldn't believe it. He didn't look happy at all but pulled it off and tucked it in his pocket.

Isabel turned to shake his hand, but Kip jumped off the podium and slithered into the crowd.

By the time December rolled around, dreams of Christmas crowded out Isabel's troubles with Grandmother Biltmore.

"Can I go out to the barn now, Mom?" she asked bright and early one morning.

"You don't want to wait for breakfast?"

Isabel shook her head and smiled. "Nah, I'm too excited for Holly's sleepover tomorrow. We have so much to do to get ready."

"Um, I think you should eat first," said Mom, taking a cheesy-egg casserole out of the oven. "Can you call your dad? It looks like this is done."

Isabel jumped off the stool and ran out on the front porch. She cupped her hands over her mouth. "Da-ad! Come and get it!" She turned around, slammed the door shut, and rushed back into the kitchen.

Mom raised her eyebrows. "I could have done that myself. I was hoping you would *go out* and get your dad."

Isabel looked down sheepishly, "Sorry."

A few minutes later, the back door opened and in stepped the most wonderful man in the world to Isabel. "Do I smell cheesy eggs?" He grinned.

"Daddy!" Isabel ran over and hugged his neck.

Dad smooched Isabel on the cheek. "Good morning, Princess."

Isabel looked into his warm brown eyes and melted. His jet black hair was pasted down on his forehead from his hat, and his firm chin gave him that rugged look she loved so much.

Isabel chuckled to think that when she was four, she wanted to marry him someday. That is, until she found out he was *already* married — to her mother. She was brokenhearted for days until Daddy told her they would be special, best buddies instead. And so they were. They went hunting and fishing together every weekend. They galloped their horses through the grassy hills and up to Moose Lake. Isabel didn't know what she would ever do without

Dad. She couldn't even think about it for one minute.

Dad planted himself on a kitchen chair and scooped a heaping spoonful of, steamy eggs and sausage onto his plate. He looked over at Isabel. "Ready for the big sleepover tomorrow night?"

"Yep." Isabel picked up her flowered box. "I have my Christmas cards right here, all ready for our project."

Dad's eyes twinkled. "I sure hope I get one of those new place mats this year."

"I don't know," Isabel teased. "You'll have to wait and see on Christmas." She gulped down her milk. "Can I go now, Mom?"

Mom nodded.

Isabel started for the door. "Hurry up, Daddy!" she called over her shoulder with a smile. "The day's not going to wait for ya!"

Isabel trotted down to the mud room, pulled on her coat and boots, and skipped out into the chilly morning air. Tinkerbell, the barn cat, greeted her, purring against her legs.

"Mornin', Tink." She picked her up and stroked her orange-striped fur. "Look at that silvery mist floating on the mountaintop. Looks like angels." She giggled. Tink looked over at the mountaintop and meowed. "You love this place, don't you, Tinkerbell?" A sudden pain stabbed Isabel's heart when she remembered Grandmother Biltmore's troubling words: "I'm taking back the loan on the ranch."

"Dad says God always works things out for the good," Isabel said, looking at Tinkerbell. "But maybe I need to give things a little push; give God a little help." Isabel sighed. "But how?" She set Tinkerbell down.

"Nhhhh," Starlight whinnied as Isabel entered the barn and walked up to his stall. He tossed his head a little as if he was saying hello. Isabel reached out and stroked his gentle face.

"Hey, boy." The touch of his lips tickled her hand. He sniffed her coat, clearly searching for a tasty treat. "You found it," she said, "Good boy." She reached into her coat pocket and pulled out three lumps of sugar. Starlight snapped up the treat and nosed around for more.

Isabel laughed. Somehow, just being with Starlight always made her feel better. "That's all there is for now," she told him.

Isabel picked up the brush and ran it through his thick brown hair. "O come, all ye faithful," she sang in a loud, clear voice. "Joyful and triumphant! O come, ye, O come, ye, to Beth-e-th-le-hem. Come and behold Him, born the King of angels. O come, let us adore Him . . ."

"It smells like snow," Dad interrupted, poking his head into the stall. He pulled his wool jacket up around his neck and rubbed his hands together. His warm breath rose in little puffs above him. "I hope the snow holds off until your mom and I get back from Red Mountain Ranch tomorrow."

Mom walked into the barn behind him. Two little wrinkles furrowed her forehead, just like they always did when she was worried. "Looks like snow tomorrow, Sam. Lots and lots of snow." She crossed her arms.

"Yippee!" Isabel kissed Starlight's nose.

Dad was mucking out the stall. "I thought the weatherman said only flurries."

Mom gave Dad a pleading look. "You know how unpredictable Colorado weather can be. I don't want to leave Isabel alone all day if there's going to be bad weather. Maybe we should postpone our trip until next week."

"Izzy's a responsible girl," Dad said. He wrapped his arm around Isabel's shoulder. "She's almost twelve. She'll be fine here. Our trusty ranch hand, Sky, will be here tending the horses 'til three o'clock, and Mrs. Paddington lives right next door. Holly's coming to spend the night tonight. She'll keep Isabel company during the day while we're gone tomorrow. It's only a day trip. Remember, we'll be back before it gets dark."

Mom sighed and gave a half smile. "I know. You're right, Sam." She put her arm around Isabel's shoulder, right next to Dad's. "Isabel is our big girl now."

Chapter Four
Sleepover

The next morning Holly and Isabel jumped around, batting their pillows at each other as Isabel's parents drove off to buy new horses at Red Mountain Ranch. Isabel turned on Christmas music, and the girls danced around her bedroom. "What should we do first?" she asked Holly.

"Make chocolate confetti!" said Holly, diving on the bed. "I brought over these cute Chinese boxes with pink angels on them. We can fill them with the candy and tie curly silver ribbons all around the handles."

Thank you, God, for Holly, Isabel prayed. *She's my connection with the girl world.* She grinned inwardly when she remembered how helpful Holly could be. She'd helped Isabel fix her hair for the spring play last year. Everyone told Isabel how pretty she looked. Even if the recent secret weapon *had* failed, it wasn't Holly's fault. *Mom always says Holly is a good influence on me.*

All Isabel knew was that Holly was the best friend a girl could ever have.

"Race ya!" shouted Isabel. The giggling girls sprinted down the stairs in their nightgowns and slid across the kitchen floor in their socks. "The mixing bowl and spoon are in the strainer," she instructed. She opened the cabinets and rummaged around for the ingredients for the chocolate confetti. "What did you get me for Christmas?" she asked.

Her friend smiled. "You'll have to wait for Christmas Eve to find out." Holly's golden hair shone in the morning light. *If she had a silver-colored, satin bow tied in her hair,* thought Isabel, *she would look like the Christmas angel on top of our tree.*

Isabel skipped over to the pantry. She stopped suddenly in front of it and stared.

"What is it?" asked Holly.

"Grandmother Biltmore's Christmas card," she said, pointing to a gold-gilded card taped to the cabinet door. Isabel pursed her lips. She pulled the card off and tucked it behind the canisters on the counter.

"Good thinking," said Holly with that comforting look.

"Hmph! I'm not going to let Gran's mean threats ruin my day."

Isabel reached in and grabbed the M&M's and pretzels. She took a deep breath and let it out slowly. Just *holding* chocolate in her hands made her feel better.

"This time *I'll* melt the chocolate," chided Holly.

An hour flew by before they noticed the gray clouds gathering outside. Isabel pressed her nose against the window and watched the white, velvety snowflakes swirl down from the sky.

"Holly, look. It's snowing. It's perfect for catching snowflakes on your tongue. Come on, let's go outside." Next to horses, Isabel loved snow. Maybe she and Holly could make snow horses to ride on.

The girls giggled as they dashed upstairs to Isabel's room to put on warm clothes. Then they pulled on their boots and coats and ran out into the swirling snow.

Holly held her arms up and twirled around with her mouth open. "Isn't it all sparkly and beautiful?"

"Wouldn't it be great if the snowflakes were chocolate?" said Isabel.

"Oh, I got one!" Holly giggled. "It tickles my tongue!"

It wasn't long before the girls' hair was powdered with snow and their cheeks were rosy with cold. Holly pulled her coat tighter around her and shivered. "It feels like it's getting a lot colder." Isabel looked around. It did feel colder. She was suddenly aware that her teeth were chattering. Her fingers felt stiff with cold, even in her mittens. Her knees began to knock.

She peered through the blowing snow as another thought came to mind. "Where's Sky's truck? He was supposed to come by today and feed the horses." Then she gasped, her frozen fingers forgotten for the moment. "Oh no! What if Starlight hasn't eaten today?"

Isabel darted toward the barn. "Come on, Holly!"

Starlight whinnied when he saw her and stomped his hoof. His breath made little clouds of smoke.

"Hey, boy." Isabel patted his head. "We didn't forget you." She pulled his blanket off the fence and put it on his back. "Is that better?" Her eyes studied the barn. "Holly, it doesn't look like any of the animals have been fed."

Holly nodded and rubbed her hands together. "I'm freezing!" she said, shivering. "Let's hurry."

"Holly, you put feed in the sheep's trough. I'll do the horses."

Isabel and Holly worked hard for the next hour giving food and water to the animals.

"Okay, all done here," called Isabel.

"Me too," said Holly through chattering teeth.

"Let's go inside."

By now, the wind was blowing so hard that Isabel and Holly could hardly open the barn door. "Push!" cried Isabel. When they pushed the door open, the entire ranch—for as far as they could see—lay covered with a thick blanket of powdery snow. The clouds and sky were so white that there was a blur between the land and sky.

"I can't see the house!" cried Holly.

Isabel grabbed Holly's hand. She could find her way around the ranch blindfolded if she had to. She hoped. "It's this way. Come on."

The girls held onto the end of the corral fence and inched their way in the direction of the house. "Over there!" cried Isabel, pointing. "I think I see the red rooster on top of the house."

Isabel and Holly clutched each other, tucked their heads down, and pushed their way toward the house.

"I can't feel my feet," Holly cried.

"Don't stop!" shouted Isabel. "We're almost there."

Isabel's breath was coming in small gasps by the time the girls stumbled up the stairs of the back porch and through the kitchen door. With a moan of relief, Isabel collapsed on the floor. Holly looked like she was going to cry and fell down beside her.

Isabel and Holly basked in the incredible warmth of the kitchen. Isabel felt tiny bits of icy snowflakes begin to melt. They dripped across her face and splashed onto the linoleum floor.

Finally, Isabel raised her head and sat up. She took a deep breath and shuddered. "It must be a blizzard."

Holly lay panting on the floor, whimpering.

Isabel bent down and pulled off Holly's boots.

"It's going to be okay," she said, helping her up. "Come on. Let's put on some dry clothes and make hot chocolate."

Holly was quiet. She nodded and shivered.

The girls changed out of their wet clothes and put on thick sweaters, socks, and jeans. "Maybe we better watch the weather channel," said Isabel, grabbing the remote.

"Heavy blizzard warnings in Silver Creek County," reported the announcer. "Listeners are advised to stay put and check for supplies. We may have two feet of snow by midnight."

Holly's eyes grew wide.

Isabel reached for her cell phone. "I'm calling Mom." She dialed her mom's cell. "It went straight to voice mail." She looked at Holly and bit her lip.

"Try again," coaxed Holly, shivering.

Isabel dialed again. "Now the line is busy."

Holly fell back on the kitchen chair. "What are we going to do?"

"Mom keeps a list on the inside of this cabinet on what to do in case of storms," said Isabel. As she opened the cabinet, the electricity flickered.

Holly's lip began to tremble as she peered out the window. "Hurry!" The dull, gray light of the afternoon was fading into a thick, dark night as the snow clouds covered the sky.

Isabel pulled the list off the door and read it out loud: "Turn on the radio. Batteries are on top of fridge. Tune into FM 1090 weather station." She paused.

"Go on," Holly urged.

"Get extra camping flashlights in attic," Isabel continued. "DON'T USE CANDLES. COULD START A FIRE." She caught Holly's frightened gaze and smiled. "That's good advice."

Holly nodded.

"Put on thermal underwear. Roll up towels under the doors and windows to keep out drafts. Run water into large pans to save for drinking in case pipes freeze. Turn on faucets to drip in kitchen and bathrooms to keep the pipes from freezing.

"Let's do the towels first," said Isabel. The girls darted to the linen closet and loaded their arms with towels. They rolled them up and placed them under the doors and all the windows on the first floor.

The electricity flickered again. Isabel's eyes widened. "Lord," she whispered, "show us what to do." She turned to Holly. "There's a blue thermos under the sink. Fill it with the rest of the hot chocolate while I fill some pots with water." The girls worked like a building crew as the snow and winds beat against the house.

"Sleeping bags!" cried Isabel. "They're up in the attic with the flashlights."

The girls clung to each other as they climbed the stairs. Isabel's heart banged against the inside of her chest as loudly as a galloping horse. She didn't like being without her parents at a time like this.

Something outside crashed against the house with a loud bang. Holly jumped. "What was that?"

"I don't know," said Isabel, "but let's keep going."

They opened the attic door, revealing an old rocking chair and rugs. The musty smell itched Isabel's nose. "I think the camping stuff is over here," she said, beckoning. The girls walked towards the large metal shelves in the corner and found the box marked *camping*.

"Yes!" shouted Isabel. She pulled the box down and grabbed the flashlights and camping lanterns.

She clicked them on. "They still work." Isabel dug around the box looking for batteries. "There's a bunch of batteries too. Here." She handed a flashlight to Holly. "The sleeping bags should be over there in the corner."

Holly wandered off, looking through the piles of stuff like she was shopping at a rummage sale. "Your mom sure has a lot of old junk up here. I don't see the sleeping bags," Holly called back. "Just some old blankets and a cool old trunk."

Isabel stopped what she was doing and made her way around the piles to Holly. "A cool old trunk?"

Holly opened the lid. "Yeah, look. There are tons of old pictures in it. Looks like pictures of a Native American reservation. Ever seen them?"

Isabel looked thoughtful. "I don't think so. What's my mom doing stashing an old trunk with photos up here?"

"Wow, look at the chief with all his feathers," Holly said. "Must have been some kind of ceremony."

Isabel slowly knelt beside the trunk. "I've never seen these pictures before. Miss Kittle says Native Americans are the Forgotten People. It's so sad how some of them live now."

Holly flipped through the pages.

"Wait!" cried Isabel. "I know that woman. She looks like Aunt Tabitha, the sweet Native American

woman Mom and I have tea with every month."
Isabel's mind was swirling.

"There's an envelope in here too," Holly said.
When she opened it, she turned white. "It . . . it . . . it
has a lock of hair in it and some tiny teeth. Ew!"
Holly threw the envelope down like it was
contaminated

"Don't be a scaredy-cat," teased Isabel. She
picked up the envelope and shined her light on it.
"There's a note inside." Carefully, she slipped the
note out of the envelope and unfolded it. "It's a
poem."

> *Early in the dawn*
> *A mourning dove came to call.*
> *Sweetly singing in my tent;*
> *With hair the color of night.*
> *The sun laughed, the deer leapt;*
> *My spirit sang for joy, my sweet Maya.*

Holly tilted her head. "Isn't Maya your middle
name?"

"Yeah." Goose bumps ran up Isabel's arms, and
she shivered. "I feel creepy. Put it back. Let's get the
sleeping bags and go back downstairs."

Isabel kept her thoughts to herself when they
returned to the living room. She wasn't sure what to
make of the things they found in the trunk, but she
couldn't shake the feeling that there was something
important in there.

The lights flickered again, but this time they didn't come back on. The girls grabbed each other tight. "Hang on, Holly. It's going to be all right."

Isabel flashed her light over at the plaque on the wall as they inched their way to the living room. A huge, white, glowing angel with outstretched wings covered two children in the painting. "I will abide under the shadow of the Almighty," it read, "until the storm passes by." Isabel sighed. A twinge of peace began to work its way into her soul.

She took the phone out of her pocket. "I'm trying Mom again." She nervously glanced over at Holly. "Still busy." Isabel plopped down on the couch. *Oh, how I wish Mom and Dad were here.*

"I'm scared," said Holly, sitting down next to Isabel. She crouched in the corner of the sofa and pulled the blanket up to her nose.

"Don't worry, Holly. Everything is going to be okay." *I hope everything is going to be okay!*

Holly gulped and nodded.

"I know what," said Isabel. "Let's make the Christmas card place mats we planned. Maybe it will keep our minds off of the storm."

"G-good idea," stammered Holly.

Isabel carefully felt her way over to the desk in the gloomy half-light. She grabbed her flowered box with the Christmas cards in it. Then she knelt down by Holly and spread them out on the coffee table.

"Let's turn on the radio," said Holly. The song "Jingle Bells" began to fill the room with music. Isabel gave a little smile, then Holly grinned. The girls looked at each other and laughed. "Over the fields we go," sang Isabel, "laughing all the way."

"Ha, ha, ha!" added Holly.

The girls started their project under the warm glow of the lanterns. They cut out the shapes on the Christmas cards and glued them on large sheets of green construction paper.

"This place mat is for my dad," said Isabel. She glued down a manger scene.

"Isn't baby Jesus cute in this one?" said Holly, lifting it up. "This one is for my sister, Beth."

"Mighty God, Prince of Peace," Isabel read on the next card. A deep peace enveloped her. The storm had taken her mind off Grandmother Biltmore and her threats to take away the ranch, yet there was a hope growing in her heart. *Maybe there is a way to stop her plan,* she thought, *but how?*

The hot chocolate from the thermos kept them warm, and they chattered like two little birds. Decorating the place mats had really helped calm their nerves, even if they had to do it by lantern light. *Six new Christmas gifts for Christmas Eve,* thought Isabel. *Not a bad evening after all.*

The storm continued to rage into the night, but it didn't seem scary anymore. Around eleven o'clock, the gentle music of "Silent Night" drifted from the radio. The girls looked at each other and smiled. They crawled into the sleeping bags, grabbed hands, and peacefully drifted off to sleep.

Chapter Five
Betrayed

It was dawn when Isabel heard the snowplow rumbling down the road. Rubbing her eyes, she sat up and yawned, wondering if the events of the evening were all a dream. She looked at Holly snug in her sleeping bag and the placemats that lay on the table beside her. No, it was all real. The electricity flickered on. Isabel took a deep breath. She was so happy she wanted to cry.

She dashed over to the windows and opened the shades. "Oh, gorgeous," she breathed. The sun was peeking out from the horizon with beautiful shades of pink spilling across the sky. Cupping her eyes, she tried to make out the green vehicle sloshing around behind the snowplow. *It's Mom and Dad. They're home!*

Isabel looked up. "Thank you, God. Wake up, Holly! Wake up!" Isabel danced a little jig. "We made it through the storm. We're alive!" Somehow she felt a little older, a little wiser for weathering the storm. And for being brave for Holly, her best friend in the world.

Holly sat up with her hair in a mess, still clinging to the picture of baby Jesus in the manger. "He *is* our Prince of Peace," she murmured.

By April, the cold winter had passed, and springtime burst forth with the sprinkling of purple and yellow flowers adorning the pastures. Isabel felt dreamy as she sat at her bedroom window with her head cupped in her hands. She watched three baby porcupines scuttle along after their mother among the juniper trees. Down by the pond, a group of yellow goslings waddled and dove in for their morning swim.

Isabel beamed. She loved spring, when everything was fresh and alive. She pulled on her boots then dashed downstairs and skipped out to the stable. Tinkerbell was crouched on a hay bale, watching for mice. "Hey, Tink! How's my girl this morning?"

Tinkerbell meowed and jumped down to greet her. "Let's look at the lambs together, want to?" Isabel picked her up and felt the gentle purring on her shoulder then climbed up on the railing to look over the stall. Two of the cutest baby lambs were nestled in the warm hay. "Hi, Buzz. Hi, Miss Kittle," said Isabel, opening the stall. She picked up Miss Kittle and cradled her around her shoulders.

"Morning, Daddy," called Isabel, strolling outside where he was working. "Miss Kittle and I came to visit you."

Dad was bent over a tractor with a wrench in his hand. He looked up. "Miss Kittle, is it? After your fifth-grade teacher?"

She giggled. "Yep, it's her crossed eyes."

Dad gazed at the lamb a little closer. "Well, if it doesn't resemble Miss Kittle," he said, smiling.

Mom came out to the barn with the cell phone in her hand, looking worried. "It's Mother," she said, handing it to Dad. "Please, be nice for my sake."

Dad wiped his hands on his jeans and took the cell phone. "Mother Biltmore, how are you today?" He listened for a minute and wrinkled his forehead. "Uh, huh. Now, Gertrude." His voice sounded firm, and his face turned red.

Isabel leaned in. "Dad, what is it?"

Dad waved his hand at her and pointed at the stable. He covered the phone. "We'll talk later."

Isabel put Miss Kittle back in her stall with the ewe and went over to visit Starlight. Starlight walked over and shook his head. Isabel kissed his nose. "Good morning." She picked up the brush and ran it along his shiny coat. "What is Gran up to now?"

Starlight snorted and stamped his foot.

"You don't trust her either, do you, boy?" Isabel took the bit and bridle off the hook and placed it over Starlight's nose. "Let's go for a ride."

Dad's face looked bright red when he came into the stable. He grabbed a pitchfork and started pitching hay with great gusto.

Isabel ran over and climbed on the rail, "Daddy, what is it?"

"Nothing for you to be concerned with, young lady."

Isabel gulped. *He's never called me that before.*

"I've thought about it," he said, stopping for a moment. "I'm enrolling you in Camp Tialocka this summer." He dug his pitchfork in and gave it a great heave.

"Please, Dad, no, not that! It's girl prison. They do gross stuff like make jewelry and paint each others' nails." If it's one thing that Isabel dreaded, it was going to "girl camp" with Holly. She much preferred catching frogs down at the creek or roping calves in a rodeo.

Dad stopped pitching hay and wiped the sweat off his forehead. "Holly goes there every summer. It hasn't hurt her any."

Isabel stared at her dad in disbelief. "What about CCC?"

"Colorado Cowgirl Camp can wait until next year."

"Dad, you can't mean it."

"Not another word, Izzy. Maybe your grandmother is right. A little girl time might do you some good."

Isabel felt so betrayed. *Dad is siding with Gran!* She stomped her foot and ran out of the barn with hot tears stinging her face. Charging across the yard to her tree house, Isabel jumped on the rope and scurried up. The green chair was still damp from the spring rains, but she threw herself in it anyway and crossed her arms.

"What's wrong with being a tomboy?" cried Isabel. She kicked her frog bucket. "I won't do it. I won't go. I'll run away."

Isabel wiped her nose on her shirt and stood up. She stared out over the tree house railing at the ranch she called home. The spring trees abounded with sweet blossoming flowers. Her heart melted. She couldn't help loving the way the sun danced among them. A breeze brushed over her hair. A pain pricked her chest. How could she go to Boston and leave all this?

Isabel slid down the rope. She trotted across the yard and rushed up to her bedroom, slamming the door behind her. She dove into her bed and threw the covers over her head. "I'm not going to that stupid camp," she murmured. "I don't care if Holly *does* go there and it makes me into a grand lady."

Just then she heard the front door slam and Holly's voice talking with Mom downstairs. Maybe Holly could help her think of some way she could get out of it.

A few minutes later she heard footsteps in the hall. "Hello, hello," Holly called out, knocking on the door. "Special delivery for Isabel Morningsky."

Isabel rolled over and peeked out of the covers. Her eyes were damp and swollen.

Holly gave her that "poor Izzy" look as she stood in the doorway.

Isabel sighed. Seeing Holly always made her feel better. She sat up. "Okay, come in."

Holly held out a tray with warm cinnamon rolls and two frosty glasses of milk. She set the tray down on the desk. "Izzy, what's wrong?"

Isabel folded her arms and scowled. "My dad had a fight with my grandmother on the phone today. He was so mad that the veins on his neck were popping out."

"Scary," said Holly.

"I think she's trying to get me to go back to Boston again. My dad was so mad after he talked to her. That's when he told me he wanted me to go to" — Isabel swallowed — "girl prison."

Holly jumped up, smiling. "You mean Camp Tialocka?"

Isabel felt gloomy and nodded. *How could my own father do this to me?*

"Awesome!" shouted Holly. "I promise I won't let one girl near you with nail polish. Well, no girls except me. I'll make a movie about it. It will be a big hit!"

"You know I hate that place," moaned Isabel. "It's always the same week as Cowgirl Camp. And they do all that gross girl stuff. It makes me want to throw up."

Holly crossed her arms. "It's not that bad."

"Not for you. You like that stuff."

Holly walked over to Isabel and sat on the edge of the bed. "Poor Izzy. Look at it this way. Maybe you can learn some stuff to convince your grandmother you are a lady right here in Colorado. It *almost* worked at Thanksgiving, didn't it?"

Isabel sat up and sniffed. Maybe Holly was right. "Well, sort of. I think it could have worked if I hadn't tripped on the stairs." Isabel blew her nose and wiped her eyes.

Holly held out a cinnamon roll. "Your mom made them. They're really good."

Isabel thought about what Holly said. She did hear that at camp Tialocka you could fish and hike in the wilderness. She liked that. A tiny smile hid in the corner of her mouth. She took the cinnamon roll and took a bite. "Well," she said chewing, "maybe things aren't so bad after all. "

"I rode Patches over," said Holly. "Wanna ride over to Dinosaur Creek and dig for treasure? Maybe we'll find some fossils."

Isabel licked the sweet frosting off her lips. Dinosaur Creek always made her feel better. "Yep, let's go." She grabbed her baseball cap off her bedpost, and she and Holly set out on their digging adventure.

The spring sky was robin's-egg blue, and the sweet smell of prairie grass filled the air as the girls rode over to Dinosaur Creek. Only a mile from her ranch, Dinosaur Creek was a magical place. There was always a treasure to find, a frog to catch, or an eagle to watch soaring in the blue sky.

Starlight whinnied when they rode up to the oak tree nestled on the banks of the creek. It was a special place to him too. That's where Isabel found sweet clover nestled in the grass.

Isabel dismounted and pulled off her boots and socks. She wiggled her toes. The soft green grass tickled her feet. She took a deep breath of the fresh spring air. "Last one in is a rotten egg!"

Holly smirked. "You always say that. I haven't turned into a stinky old egg yet." Holly dismounted and carefully tied up Patches. She set her boots neatly under the tree and rolled up her jeans. Then she grabbed the shovels out of her pack and skipped over to the brook. "Yikes!" Holly shivered. "The water's freezing!"

Isabel hopped across the rock path in the middle of the stream. Her dark hair blew in the breeze. She stopped and stooped down to watch a tadpole swim away. That's when she noticed a glimmering green rock on the creek bottom. A thrill of excitement rippled down her spine. *It must be a treasure!* "This looks like a good place to dig," she called back to Holly.

Holly carefully jumped across the rock path and handed Isabel a shovel. The girls plunged them into the red earth around the banks. "Maybe we'll find the lost jewels from an Indian princess," said Holly.

Isabel thrust a shovelful of dirt over her shoulder. "Or some old Apatosaurus bones." The girls hunted happily for several hours and barely noticed when the sun started to set.

Isabel stopped to survey the pile. Three arrowheads, a rock shaped like a star, and a plastic cup filled with fool's gold. "Not bad for a day's digging."

Holly tapped something with her shovel. *Clink!* "Izzy, wait! I think I found something. I can't get to it. Some rocks are blocking it. Help me."

Isabel's heart pounded with anticipation. She hurried over to dig with Holly.

Holly scraped the dirt away from the side of the object. "Whatever it is, it has writing on it."

"Keep digging!" cried Isabel. The girls shoveled harder and harder, unearthing a big clod of mud with a mysterious clay pot lodged inside. Isabel blinked and gazed at it. "This could be a *real* treasure. Let's put it in the creek!"

The girls whisked the big dirt blob over to the middle of the creek and held it under the water. The current splashed this way and that. They washed away the mud on the clay pot. "Whoa!" said Isabel, sitting back.

"It's beautiful!" cried Holly. "Have you ever seen such a pretty clay pot?"

Isabel admired the pot. "I love the stars and deer on it."

"And that blazing orange color!"

"I can't read the writing," said Isabel, wiping away the rest of the dirt. "It must be written in some Native American language."

Holly bent down to rinse off her hands. "We could take it to the Native American Museum in town and see if they know what it says."

Isabel picked up the pot and cradled it as if it were a baby. "Holly, this is something big," she said. "Really big; I feel it."

Chapter Six
The Museum

In the early morning hours, low, rumbling clouds
moved across the horizon and settled on the ranch.
Strong gusts of wind broke off a tree branch,
knocking it against the house and waking Isabel. She
sat up in bed and rubbed her eyes. It was 4:00 AM.
She could hear her parents' voices trailing down the
hall.

Mom was crying. "I won't let my mother do this,
Sam. Isabel belongs here with us."

Isabel frowned and jumped out of bed. She *had* to
hear what they were saying. She carefully crept
down the hall to listen. Dad's deep voice sounded
worried. "Your mother said she will revoke the loan

on our ranch unless we let Isabel go to Boston. You know her, Grace. She's as stubborn as a mule. We'll be homeless."

Isabel didn't like hearing words like "homeless." She couldn't remember a time before the ranch. Isabel clenched her fist. *How could Gran be so mean? I'm never calling her Gran again!* She slid down the wall, sat on the carpet, and rested her head in her hands.

"Maybe we should tell Isabel the truth," said Mom, sniffling.

"We promised we wouldn't."

The words hit Isabel like a hammer. Why would her parents keep a secret from her? Didn't Dad say she could always tell him *anything?* So, why couldn't *he* tell her anything? That icky feeling of betrayal felt like a heavy rock in the pit of her stomach. *It must be something so terrible that wild horses couldn't drag it from him,* thought Isabel. A lump rose up in her throat and she stood to her feet.

Isabel paced back and forth in the hallway. They couldn't lose the ranch. Not because of her. Maybe Boston wouldn't be so bad. Maybe. She bit her lip. Who was she kidding? Gran would dress her up in scratchy chiffon dresses and curl her hair so she looked like a poodle. Isabel sighed. And how could she leave Starlight?

She heard her mom crying again. Isabel's heart felt like it was breaking. *Lord, please help me! I don't know what to do.* She couldn't help it. That still, small voice echoed loud and clear, *"Winners never quit and quitters never win, for I serve the mighty God that lives deep within."* Isabel wasn't sure how she shouldn't quit, but it seemed right that she should give back to her parents for all the things that they had given to her.

She stopped pacing. She knew what she had to do. She gave a little knock on their door and poked her head into their room. "Mom, Dad."

Mom was sitting on the bed, wiping her eyes. "Isabel, we didn't know you were up."

"I've been thinking," started Isabel. "I want to go to Grandmother Biltmore's private school."

Dad stood up. "What? Izzy, you can't be serious."

Isabel rocked back and forth and clasped her hands behind her. "Someday I will be all grown up and will want" — she gulped hard — "to get married and stuff." She hoped God would forgive her for telling a half truth, since saving the ranch was a good cause and all. She didn't know what else to do.

Mom walked over to her with sad eyes and put her arm around her. "Boston's so far away, honey."

Isabel tried to be brave. "We can call all the time and Skype. Who knows? Maybe it will be fun." Isabel had a sinking feeling. She didn't really believe it. Her lip started to quiver. "Isn't it time for breakfast?" She turned and quickly darted out of the room.

Isabel picked at her French toast. Even though it was her favorite, her heart was heavy as she ate. The bread felt like big globs of tar in her mouth.

Mom cleared the table. "Are you and Holly still riding over to the Native American Museum this morning?"

"Oh, yeah, I almost forgot." *Maybe the pot will be worth a million dollars,* thought Isabel. *Then I can buy the ranch and we won't need Grandmother Biltmore's stinky old money.* "Can I go out and saddle up Starlight?"

"Okay, come here first." Mom looked like she was going to cry again. She reached down and hugged Isabel for an extra-long time. "You're my girl, Isabel."

Isabel hugged her back for a long time. "I love you, Mom."

A gentle rain was falling when Isabel climbed up in the tree house and opened the chest where she and Holly had hidden the clay pot. She carefully held it on her lap as if it might break and watched over the railing for Holly to come. She had heard about lots of people finding fossils around town. She couldn't remember if they were worth a lot of money or not.

At last she heard the sound of horse's hooves galloping up the road. Isabel set the pot down and leaned over the rail. "Holly! Up here!"

Holly tied Patches up and dashed over to the tree house and shimmied up the ladder. "My mom said there were tons of Indian tribes in these parts for hundreds of years," she said, wide-eyed. "We Googled it last night."

"Go on."

"Some of these pots are worth thousands of dollars if you sell them on eBay."

Isabel's face lit up. "Whoa! I think my dad knows people on the reservation. Come on, let's ask him what he thinks."

Dad was in the corral, saddling up the new appaloosa he had bought at Red Mountain Ranch. Isabel and Holly trotted over and jumped up on the fence.

"Daddy, we need your help," called Isabel.

Dad tightened the girdle on the horse and walked over to them. "Anything for my little filly," he said, smiling.

Isabel held out the pot. "Look what Holly and I found down at Dinosaur Creek."

Dad's face turned white. He squirmed like his shirt was scratchy and rubbed his forehead.

"It has some writing on it, but we can't figure it out. Do you think the people you know on the reservation could tell us what it says?"

Dad's voice sounded strained and he fidgeted. "Where did you find it?"

"It was buried in the banks at the creek. It was lodged in." Isabel pushed her shoulders back and stood up tall. "But winners never quit, and quitters never win. So we dug with all of our might 'til we pulled it out."

"Yep, that's right, Mr. M.," said Holly, smiling. "We're going over to the Native American Museum in town today to see if they know anything."

Dad was silent for a minute and looked up towards the sky like he was searching for something. He kicked at the pebbles on the ground. "Maybe that's a good idea," he said finally. "If they don't know anything, we can take it to the reservation. Will you let me know what you find out?"

Isabel nodded.

Isabel wrapped a scarf around the clay pot to make sure it was safe and placed it in her saddle bag. Somehow she felt it held a special meaning, and she was determined to find out what it was.

The girls mounted their horses. "Okay, Holly, let's ride," said Isabel. She gave Starlight a gentle nudge. The clouds gently sprinkled rain on them while they trotted across the pasture, laughing on their way to the museum.

Holly tucked her hair neatly under her hat so she wouldn't get it wet. Not Isabel. She loved the adventure of the wind and rain in her hair. *It feels wonderful!*

"Let's race," said Isabel, "before it pours."

Holly grinned. "You're on!"

The girls gave their horses a kick and off they raced through the field of purple clover.

There was something about the smell of leather saddle soap and the earthy scent of Starlight's mane that gave Isabel a thrill. She felt like she was in the Kentucky Derby. She bent down and whispered in Starlight's ear, "I'll give you extra carrots if you beat Patches today." Starlight tossed his head and whinnied. Then he bolted off like a flash.

The girls leaned over and squinted at each other, urging their horses to run faster. Starlight darted ahead and reached the oak tree first. "That a boy," Isabel congratulated him.

Holly trotted up from behind. "Wow! Starlight ran like lightning. What are you feeding him?"

Isabel smiled and ran her hand along his black mane. "Only a few extra carrots, right, boy?" Isabel knew the real reason he ran faster. It was because he loved her and liked winning as much as she did.

The rain stopped, and a sunbeam peeked out from behind the clouds. A beautiful rainbow appeared above the mountains and arched across the sky.

"Izzy, look! How pretty!" exclaimed Holly.

Goose bumps ran up Isabel's spine. She looked at Holly. "I think it's a sign. What if the pot is worth a lot of money?"

"What would you do with your half?" asked Holly.

"I'd buy our ranch," Isabel blurted out.

Holly stopped and looked at her. "Why?"

"Oh, no reason." She felt so terrible and embarrassed about losing the loan. It was all her fault for not being ladylike enough. She couldn't tell Holly, not yet.

"What about you?" asked Isabel, changing the subject as quickly as she could.

Holly put her finger up to her chin. "Hmm . . . let me think." Then her face lit up. "I would buy Camp Tialocka!"

Isabel took the clay pot out of her saddle bag and cradled it like a baby. "Well, this is it." She ambled up the stone steps with Holly towards the door. A big black bear on a totem pole towered above it. Isabel felt like she was in a dream. What secrets about the pot lay beyond those doors? Butterflies tickled her stomach. "There's something wonderful about his pot, Holly."

Opening the door to the Native American museum was like slipping through a portal into another world. Three buffalo-skin teepees — adorned with sun and deer — camped in the middle of the room.

"It all looks so real," said Holly.

Isabel set the pot down and crossed her arms, uttering in a husky voice. "Maybe Little Deer will come and cook buffalo for Chief Big Feather's dinner."

The girls looked at each other and giggled.

Holly dashed over to a glass case filled with jewelry. "Oh, Izzy, look," she cooed. "The turquoise necklaces are so bea-u-ti-ful! There are rings and bracelets too. The tag says: 'Made by the tribes of the American Southwest.'"

Isabel gazed around in amazement, gliding her hand over the stuffed eagles and bears as she walked. "Look at the papoose-carrying thingies on the wall," she called to Holly. She read the sign out loud: "Native American Cradleboards. Used to keep a baby safe, much like an American snuggly." Isabel was enchanted. "I love the moon and stars painted on them. It makes me think of how the night sky is all aglow with stars on the ranch."

"Izzy, look!" Holly stood next to a display that held dozens of pipes with nature carvings on them. She crossed her arms and spoke with a raspy voice, "You smoke'em peace pipe?"

Isabel chuckled from across the room. "Now, all you have to do is braid your hair and dye it black."

Holly strolled over to the counter and opened a photo album. "Whoa, Izzy, you gotta see this. The photos are like ones we saw in the attic."

Isabel trotted over and stood next to Holly as she slowly turned the pages.

"This girl kinda looks like you," Holly said, pointing. "Heap big Isabel Messy Hair!" She chuckled.

"Very funny."

A short, dark-haired woman with high cheekbones walked over to them. "Looks like you two have an old Ute Indian clay pot."

"The Ute?" Isabel said, eyes wide.

"Yes. The Ute Indians lived all over these parts hundreds of years ago near Cripple Creek Canyon, in the shadow of the Red Mountain. It's called Pikes Peak today." The woman smiled. "They have a big reservation about sixty miles from here."

Isabel handed the pot to her. "Can you tell us what it says?"

The woman put her glasses on. "Well, let me see." She turned it around and around and then smiled. "It's a poem celebrating the birth of a baby."

Holly looked at Isabel and swallowed. "Does the poem start off: 'Early in the dawn'?"

"Why yes," said the woman, looking surprised. "I thought you didn't know what it said."

Isabel glared at Holly. "Uh, we don't. Just a lucky guess."

"Some of the next lines are too faded to read. But the last line reads: 'My spirit sang for joy, my sweet Maya.' There's a date on it, too," said the woman. "Let me see. It looks like October . . . something . . .1998."

Isabel stood frozen and stared at Holly.

The woman looked over her glasses. "Is something wrong, dear?"

"Uh, no ma'am," said Holly, grabbing Isabel's hand. "We just need to get home for dinner." She pulled Isabel towards the door. "Thank you for everything," she called over her shoulder.

When the two girls stepped outside, Isabel's knees buckled and she collapsed on the bench. Her heart was pounding and she swallowed. She stared up at the totem pole with the bear carved on top. "I feel creepy, Holly. What does all this mean?"

Holly sat down beside her. "Maybe it's just a freaky coincidence that you were born in the same month and the same year," she said. "What if you had a twin who died or something, or who was whisked away by Indians in the night?"

Isabel raised her eyebrows. "You read too many books."

"What about the story we read in the newspaper last year about the child who was found on the reservation, crying in the woods? No one knew where he came from or who his parents were."

Isabel didn't know what to think. Her head was swimming with ideas. What if the name on the pot was a cousin or what if Holly was right? Maybe *she* was the lost child wandering around the reservation and her parents adopted her. Isabel put her hand to her head to steady herself. This was all too much to think about!

"Maybe Dad knows something," she murmured. "One thing I know for sure, we need to get home right away and start a clue book. There's something fishy going on here, and we need to find out what it is."

Chapter Seven
Camp Tialocka

When June 15th arrived, Dad stood by his decision to send Isabel to camp Tialocka. "I'll muck out the stalls for a month," Isabel begged. "I won't play on online for the whole summer. You can take away my MP3 player."

"Nope, not budging," said Dad with his lips pressed together. "You're going, and that's final." Dad looked at her with those chocolate eyes that melted her heart. "Maybe I've given in to you too much, Izzy. I love having you do things with me on the ranch, but maybe I'm being selfish. Maybe it's time for the girl inside to come out."

For the first time in her life, Isabel was speechless. She couldn't believe her ears. She just stood there staring. Was Dad giving in to Gran? What was this irritating feeling eating her deep down inside? Could Dad be right? Isabel tried to shake it off and trudged off to bed.

The next morning Isabel lay in her bed staring at the ceiling. Why was her dad doing this to her? He knew she hated girl stuff. "Grrr!" She picked up a pillow and threw it across the room. *What am I going to do?* Soon she would be riding that horrible yellow school bus off to her doom. *How will I ever survive?*

All of a sudden, Isabel remembered the Bible verse from the Sunday school lesson yesterday. "I can do all things through Christ who strengthens me." She sighed. "I don't think I can get through this week without you, Lord. Please show me the way and give me strength."

Isabel rolled over and flipped opened her clue book to study it one more time.

Blizzard Day- Found poem in attic about a baby named Maya, along with creepy hair and teeth. Do my parents know the parents of this baby? Did the baby die?

April. 16 - Found cool American Indian clay pot down at Dinosaur Creek with same poem written on it. It was stuck deep inside the mud, but Holly and I dug it out.

*April 20- Went to the American Indian Museum.
Poem was the same as the one in the attic. Date on it was
almost the same as my Birthday. Freaky!*

*April 20- Later that day, Mom and Dad acted weird
when I asked them about it. Said they didn't know
anything. But the way Mom looked at Dad was sad. They
quickly changed the subject and left the room. Highly
suspicious!*

"Hmm . . ." Isabel put the pencil to her chin and
stared out the window. "I've got to uncover
Grandmother Biltmore's terrible secret and spoil her
plan," she said with determination. "Maybe if I
figure this out, I won't have to go to Boston. After
all, winners never quit and quitters never — "

"The bus is here!" Mom's voice interrupted.

"Be right down."

Isabel closed her book and buried it deep inside
her blue-jean duffle bag. She picked up her baseball
cap and plopped it on her head then trotted down
the stairs to what she was sure would be a miserable
fate.

It was a good thing Isabel had brought her MP3
player on the bus. The other girls sang silly camp
songs all the way to Camp Tialocka. Even though

she turned the volume up on high she could still hear them. *They sound like a pack of sick hyenas.*

"No, you can't get to heaven on your roller skates," sang the girls. "No, you can't get to heaven on your roller ska-a-ates. No, you can't get to heaven on your roller skates; you'll skate right past those pearly gates. All my sins are washed away, I've been redeemed!"

Isabel looked sympathetically over at Holly, who had a sappy grin on her face. *The poor girl's a goner. How does she survive all this?*

At last the yellow school bus rumbled up the gravel driveway to Camp Tialocka and came to a halt. A surprising look of delight lit up Isabel's face. Twelve rustic pine cabins sat on the banks of a shimmering lake. *There must be tons of frogs in that lake,* she thought excitedly. *Who could I get to go frogging with me?* She eagerly looked around.

Hmm, Holly's a definite no. She looked across at a redheaded girl with a fresh French manicure. *Curly Sue won't want to ruin her nails.* Next to Isabel sat a quiet girl who was frightened by a bee on the bus. Isabel shook her head. No, the poor girl would probably have nightmares for a week. *Blondy, with the designer shorts? No, she won't want to get them dirty.*

Isabel sighed. She remembered that verse again. *I can do all things through Christ who strengthens me.* She wasn't so sure about that.

The bus driver opened the door, and the gang of giggling girls shuffled off the bus in flowered shorts and flip-flops.

At least the air is fresh, thought Isabel as she stepped off behind them. A mourning dove flew overhead and cooed. She grabbed the binoculars out of her backpack to get a closer look. "So cool..." She sighed.

"I can't wait to make jewelry," said the blonde-haired girl, bumping her from behind.

"Hel-lo!" snapped Isabel. "Watch where you're going."

The blonde girl shrugged her shoulders and put her hand over her mouth. "Oh, my bad." She flipped her hair and kept on walking.

Isabel gave Holly an angry look and shook her head. Maybe she could catch the bus driver before he left.

Holly reached out and touched Isabel's shoulder. "You're going to like it, Izzy, I promise."

At 6:00 AM the next morning, Isabel was awakened by the shrill sound of a bugle. "No," she groaned, rolling over. She reached for the pillow and covered her head. "Please let this be a bad dream."

Holly shook her bunk. "Izzy, wake up. I'm so excited! Today we meet all the other tribes and get our patches."

Isabel squinted at her friend and swiped her dark mop of hair out of her eyes.

Holly frowned. "Yikes, maybe I can do your hair this morning."

"My hair is just fine," said Isabel, flattening it down with her hand. Why was Holly always worried about her hair?

Holly started jiggling the bed. "You're here, you're finally here!" she squealed.

"Hey, where'd everyone go?" asked Isabel, looking around.

"To breakfast," said Holly. "And you're late. You better hurry if you want pop tarts."

Isabel noticed that Holly was dressed in baby-blue, plaid shorts and a blue tank top. It looked like she'd spent the last hour fixing her blonde curls in an elaborate French braid with tiny blue flowers woven in. "You look like a mermaid," Isabel teased.

"Why, thank you." said Holly, bowing.

Isabel slipped on her jean shorts and threw on her baseball cap. "I'm ready." She held out her arm. "Now, lead me to the pop tarts."

After breakfast and saying the camp pledge, the girls sat at long wooden tables and strung colorful beads and trinkets together to make jewelry.

Miss Kittle, with her thick, black glasses, walked back and forth among the group to instruct them. . Isabel thought she looked like a friendly owl. *It's fun having your school teacher as your camp counselor.* "The Native Americans were very industrious," informed Miss Kittle. "They used things they found in nature to make jewelry, like beads, stones, and seeds. Today we're including some modern-day crystal beads and ornaments, as well."

Isabel held up her wrist and admired the turquoise bracelet she made. "This is actually pretty cool." *Maybe everything about girl's camp isn't so bad.*

Holly took a long time counting and recounting beads. Then she lined them up perfectly and strung them all together.

"What did you make?" asked Isabel. "Let me see."

Holly held up a beautiful, pink-beaded necklace with a crystal bluebird dangling from the center. The bluebird matched Holly's blue eyes perfectly. She reached around her neck and tied it on. It was a tradition that each girl be given a camp name before she left that week. "What do you think about 'Bluebird' for my camp name?"

"I like it. I'll vote for that."

Holly put her hands on her hips and tilted her head. "Now, we need a nickname for you."

"How about Crow Head?" blurted the girl with bleached blonde hair from the other end of the table. The four girls at the end of the table formed what Isabel called the Snob Mob. They looked at Isabel and snickered.

Isabel stood up and glared at them. Holly reached out and grabbed Isabel's arm. "That's Amanda Parkington. Don't listen to her. She thinks she's all that."

A girl with frizzy hair sitting across the table sighed. "She *is* all that."

Miss Kittle adjusted her glasses. "Tomorrow we will learn archery and survival skills in the woods."

A fire rose in Isabel's chest. "We'll see how well Little Miss *Bark*-ington can survive in the woods."

The next morning Isabel sat up front during survival class with Miss Kittle.

"Everyone stand and face this way." Miss Kittle pointed. "This is north. The sun rises in the east and sets in the west. Now, stretch out your arms."

Amanda was sitting behind Isabel and poked her in the back with her arm.

"Ouch!" Isabel cried out.

"Oh, sorry," said Amanda, in a prissy voice. "My bad."

"It's a shame you don't understand instructions," said Isabel. "Miss Kittle said arms at your side." Isabel motioned with her arms.

Amanda sneered. "Whatever."

"If you are facing north," continued Miss Kittle, "then the east is always on the right, the west is always on your left, and the south behind you. Would someone come up to demonstrate with me?"

Holly raised her hand.

No, Holly, don't! Isabel cringed. Holly was notorious for getting lost.

Miss Kittle held up a ball. "Okay, Holly, this ball is your east. Which arm would you put in that direction?"

Holly put out her left arm. "Oh, I'm confused," she said and turned in a circle. The class giggled.

Isabel ran up to rescue Holly. She stuck out her right arm for Holly to see. "Your right arm would point to the east."

"Then which way is north?" asked Miss Kittle.

Isabel turned her body so that her right arm was pointing toward the ball. "The way I'm facing is north."

"And south?"

"Behind me."

"That's correct, Isabel. Good job. You girls can sit down."

"Thanks," whispered Holly with a half-smile.

"No problem."

"If you know which direction your camp is when you set out, then you will always know how to find your way back."

The room of girls looked at each other with relief.

"Before you leave today, I have a surprise," added Miss Kittle.

A happy chatter arose from the group.

"What is it? What is it, Miss Kittle?" asked a girl with braces.

"This spring we added a stable with horses. It's just outside the camp. We're going on trail rides."

A shout rose among the girls.

"And for those of you who are better riders," added Miss Kittle, "we will be playing horse games with the camp across the lake."

Isabel and Holly looked at each other, beaming. "Horse games!" squealed Holly.

"More campers?" groaned Isabel.

"I think you will like *these* campers," said Holly. "They all like rock climbing and fishing and boy stuff like that."

Isabel felt giddy. "You mean a camp for tomboys? Holly Haddleburg, why haven't you told me about this before?"

"No silly, they *are* boys!"

Isabel thought for a minute. "That's cool." She got along well with boys.

Isabel couldn't wait to get out of the stuffy meeting room and into the fresh summer air. She wanted to hike over to the stables.

When Isabel got to the stables, Amanda was complaining as usual. "These horses are smelly," she said, holding her nose.

The horses poked their heads out of their stalls, curious to see what all the noise was about.

"Be quiet, Amanda," said Isabel. "You'll frighten them." How could anyone not like the smell of horses? It reminded her of home. She strolled by each horse one by one, approaching them carefully and letting them smell her hand. She stopped at a stall that held a beautiful paint horse. Above the door, the nameplate read "Shiloh." The horse nudged her looking for a treat. "Hey, girl, wanna go for a ride?"

Shiloh whinnied softly and shook her mane.

"I see you've found a friend," said Miss Kittle, walking up behind her.

Isabel looked at Miss Kittle pleadingly. "Can I take her for a ride?"

Miss Kittle consulted her watch. "At two-thirty, Camp Rockalocka from across the lake will arrive. Because their camp has a Native American theme like ours, they wanted to do a pow wow for us today. We will ride tomorrow. Can you wait until then?"

Isabel nodded "yes" and smiled at Miss Kittle, even though her heart said "no." She was homesick, and this was a glimmer of hope.

Chapter Eight
Jason Twofeathers

When two-thirty that afternoon arrived, what Miss Kittle said came true. Canoes overflowing with eleven- and twelve-year-old boys clad in buckskins with red-and-blue face paint glided up to the banks of Camp Tialocka. Bounding out of their canoes into the water, the boys waded up to the shore, laughing and making loud animal calls.

A group of giggling girls hid behind the wide pine trees to spy on them.

"That's Jason Twofeathers," said the girl with frizzy hair, pointing. "Some say he is a real Native American.

Jason Twofeathers did look every bit like a Native American in his buckskin. His straight, raven-black hair clung to his shoulders, and he had warm, brown, laughing eyes.

Isabel suddenly had a wonderful idea. *I wonder if he wants to go frogging.*

"Izzy, this is so exciting, "Holly said, running over to her." It's like the Old Wild West!"

Isabel felt a stirring of excitement too.

"Look at those silly boys," complained Amanda. "It was a wonder they can make it up to the camp at all, the way they wrestle and throw pinecones at each other."

"I think I'll join them," said Isabel, smirking. She bent down and picked up three pinecones. "This will be fun."

Isabel sneaked behind a tree and zeroed in on the boy, Jason Twofeathers, who seemed to be the leader. She chucked the pinecones at him, one after the other.

"Ah!" Jason cried. He fell to the ground and rolled into the nearby bushes for cover.

Isabel's heart pounded. She crouched behind the pine tree and chuckled. Then she peeked out to see what the boy would do.

"Whoa!" Isabel ducked just in time. Two pinecones whizzed past her head like torpedoes.

Jason Twofeathers took a stance out in the open with his legs apart and his arms folded, looking in her direction.

Isabel came out and did the same.

"Good arm!" Jason shouted.

"Thanks. You too," she called back.

The boy's counselor, Mr. Grizzle, was a stocky man with an eagle-feathered headdress. He climbed up the hill and called them all to order. "Braves of Camp Rock-a-locka . . . assemble!"

A red-headed boy with freckles sat down in the middle of the group and began to beat a deerskin drum.

"This is it!" crowed Holly. The girls ran over in their flowered shorts and flip-flops and sat cross-legged in a circle around the boys. "Some of these boys are real Native Americans from the reservation," she whispered. "Maybe one of *them* knows a girl named Maya."

Isabel fidgeted. She wasn't so sure she wanted to know.

"Girls of Camp Ti-a-locka," announced the leader. "The boys of Camp Rock-a-locka welcome you!" The drums beat louder and faster.

Loud squeals of cheering rose from the girls. The boys stood up and started to dance in a circle.

"I love this time of year," sighed the girl with frizzy hair. "It's like we're on the Oregon Trail or something."

"Me too," said Holly with a sappy grin on her face. "Makes me want to make soap or candles or something."

When the dance ended, the boys dashed into the crowd and handed each girl a Native American patch.

Jason Twofeathers made a beeline for Isabel. He smiled at her and flipped his shiny, black hair out of his eyes. "Welcome to camp."

Isabel looked at the patch. It had a beautiful paint horse on it with feathers. "Wow, thanks." It meant more to her than she could even say.

"It figures Injun boy would give Crow Head a patch," teased Amanda.

Isabel doubled up her fist. "I oughta —"

"Don't bother, Izzy," said Holly holding her back. "Beat her at something else," she whispered. "Remember, *horse games* and *survival skills* are tomorrow."

Isabel took a deep breath, "You're right."

The next day when the sun rose, Isabel could hardly wait for the horse games. After breakfast they hiked in the woods. Amanda complained all the way.

"I wonder why she is even here," Holly griped to Isabel.

"Maybe her parents sent her here to learn some manners."

When they arrived at the stables a half hour later, Isabel was relieved to see Amanda go off on a trail ride with half of the camp girls.

The rest of the horses were penned in the corral. "Okay, girls, pick your horses," said the camp horse director.

Isabel scampered up to Shiloh. She whinnied. "Hi, girl." Isabel reached out her hand to let Shiloh sniff her again. Then she ran her hand along her sides and back, talking softly to her.

"I think she likes you," said the director. "She's a beauty, isn't she?"

Isabel agreed.

"I'm Miss Morgan. I own an equestrian center near Misty Springs."

"I'm from Misty springs," Isabel said.

Miss Morgan smiled. "Mount up and take your place near the fence."

Kids all around were mounting their horses. Holly seemed lost in the crowd. Isabel couldn't see her anywhere.

Just then, Jason rode by on a sleek appaloosa.

"You did great in the archery contest yesterday," Isabel called.

"Thanks! I'm an even better rider,"" He grinned.

Isabel smiled. "We'll see about that." She tightened her grip on the reins and concentrated.

Excitement coursed through her veins. There was nothing Isabel liked better than a good challenge.

"First round of musical cones," said Miss Morgan. "Play the music!"

Music blared from the loud speakers, and the riders trotted around the ring. When the music stopped, riders jumped off their horses as fast as they could and led them to the center of the ring to stand by an orange cone. The rider left without a cone was out and had to leave the ring.

It came down to three riders, including Isabel and Jason. The music played loudly while the horses trotted around the ring. When the music stopped, the three remaining contestants jumped off and pulled their horses' reins toward the middle to get to the cones. Jason's horse got spooked by a snake, so he was out. Now, it was down to the redheaded girl in braces named Elizabeth and Isabel.

Isabel bent down and whispered into Shiloh's ears. "Come on, girl, I'll get you some carrots." Shiloh pricked up her ears.

Isabel adjusted her baseball cap and rode Shiloh to the fence. Her hands were sweaty; her heart thumped wildly. "Easy girl."She steadied her horse and waited for the music to begin . . . one more time. *This is it!*

Elizabeth gazed over at Isabel and held her horse steady. The music began, and the girls cantered around the ring.

Isabel could hear the horses clomping on the clods of dirt under them, the tinkling of the bridles, and her horse's breath. The hot summer heat made her bare legs stick to the saddle.

The music stopped.

Isabel and Elizabeth jumped down from their horses and bolted for the cones. Shiloh didn't need to be pulled. She trusted Isabel as her herd leader and ran alongside her, beating Elizabeth to the cone by inches.

"We did it, Shiloh!" cried Isabel, hugging her around the neck. Shiloh nuzzled her back. Isabel's heart melted. She had made her first real camp friend.

As Isabel led Shiloh back to the stable, Holly hobbled up. "Where were you?" Isabel asked. "I won first place." Her eyes widened. "Are you okay?"

"I twisted my ankle during volleyball."Holly winced. "It's not too bad." She limped alongside Isabel.

Amanda was leaning against the fence with a group of girls as they passed by.

"Injuns should be banished from the camp," she said to another girl in a loud, snooty voice. It was obvious she wanted Isabel to hear her remark.

Isabel stopped and glared at Amanda. "What's wrong with Native Americans? They were here first."

Amanda looked at Isabel with her piercing green eyes. "It figures you wouldn't know." She flipped her blonde hair over one shoulder and strode away with the Snob Mob following right behind her.

"People like that make me so angry," said Isabel.

"People like that are just ignorant," said Holly. "Don't listen to her. Besides, I think she's jealous. Cami told me . . . that Zoe told her . . . that last year Jason gave *her* a patch and they were camp buddies. I think she was hoping that he would give it to her again this year. But instead, he gave it to you."

"Big deal," said Isabel. "That girl annoys me."

When the girls returned to the main campground, Isabel felt like she needed to get away for a while to someplace quiet.

Holly strolled up the path towards her, clipping her flip-flops.

"Hey, your ankle is better," said Isabel.

"Yep. Wanna go get an ice-cream bar? Later, Miss Kittle is going to show us what plants to eat if we get lost in the woods."

"No, thanks. I already know what plants to eat. I'm going to go for a walk in the woods."

Holly smiled. "Okay. I'll see you later."

Down on the path at the edge of the woods, Amanda Parkington and the Snob Mob guarded the road like soldiers.

Isabel froze when she saw them. *I can do all things through Christ who strengthens me,* ran through her mind. "Okay, Lord," she squeaked out, "here I go." She took a deep breath and pressed on.

When Isabel drew near, Amanda jumped in front of her like a creepy black cat. "I saw that you won the horse games today," she mocked. Amanda waved for the Snob Mob to come over.

"Yeah," said the girl with black braids and sunburn cheeks. "We have a present for you."

"It's a winner's crown," taunted Amanda.

"That's right," said another girl in the group. "It's a crown of bugs! " She reached from behind her back and dumped a can of brown, wiggly bugs on Isabel's head.

Amanda laughed. "Crow Head has a new hairdo."

Recognizing some bugs her dad said she could eat if she ever needed to survive, she reached up and popped one in her mouth. "Thank you," said Isabel, crunching.

"Eeeeew!" shrieked Amanda. She leaped back. "You're gross!"

"Yum!" said Isabel, rubbing her stomach. "I would feel bad if I didn't share. Here!" She reached up and grabbed a handful of bugs out of her hair. Then she threw them on the girls.

"Get 'em off me!" shouted the girl with braids, shaking.

Amanda had already taken off, racing down the path, "I'm telling Miss Kittle!"

The rest of the Snob Mob followed her, screaming and swiping off the bugs as they hurried back towards camp.

Isabel's heart was pounding like she had just fought a great battle. She fell against a tree trunk and slid down on the ground. "Yuck!" she muttered, spitting out the bug. "That'll teach Miss Smarty-Pants *Bark*-ington!" Isabel wiped her mouth and looked down. "Poor bug."

When Isabel finally reached the woods, she savored the cool and quiet. Yellow and blue butterflies fluttered around the bushes. She took a deep breath and sighed. She could actually hear something other than constant talking and giggling.

A redwing blackbird called out, and the locusts were starting to hum. Each bush and tree she walked by felt like old friends. She felt so relieved to be among them.

When the sun started to set, Isabel realized she had walked several miles from camp. "Uh-oh," she said, turning around in circles. "I think I'm lost." She looked for the sun and remembered that the camp was east. She heard the call of a bullfrog to its mate. *The stream will lead me back to camp!*

As she approached the stream, she heard a strange bird calling. A thrill of excitement washed over her. "I've never heard that one before. I wonder what it is. "

Isabel drew closer to the tree and looked up. The sound came from right above her. It called out even louder. She strained her eyes to see through the leafy branches, when all of a sudden a boy jumped down right in front of her.

"Ah!" shouted Isabel, stumbling backwards. "You scared me half to death!"

"Sorry," he said with a big grin. "Nice horse patch." It was Jason Twofeathers.

Isabel was glad to see him.

Even without the face paint, Jason looked like a true Native American Indian. His high cheek bones gave him that rugged look, and his nose was slightly curved.

"Wanna see something cool?" he asked.

Isabel shrugged. "Sure."

Jason jumped up like he had springs in his legs, grabbed the lowest tree branch, and hoisted himself up. He reached out his hand to Isabel. "Come on!"

Isabel scurried up the tree. She loved the shady canopy of leaves and imagined what it would be like to be a bird and live in a tree like this. She couldn't believe how quietly Jason moved as he climbed. It was as if someone had pushed the mute button on the remote.

Isabel's foot snapped a twig.

"Shhh, look." Jason pointed. He motioned for her to sit down. Crouching down next to her, he grabbed his knees. "It's a dipper's nest," he whispered. "The mother has a pile of eggs. I found it this morning."

Isabel loved birds. "Wow, that is so cool, Jason."

"You know my name?"

"Everyone knows the champion archer's name," she chided.

"You seem so different from all the other girls."

Isabel fidgeted. "I know, I —"

"I like it," he interrupted. "I get so tired of all the giggling."

"Me too." She sighed. *Okay, Isabel, ask him!* "Do you want to go frogging?" She gulped.

"That would be great," replied Jason. "In the morning?"

Isabel nodded. "Can I ask you something? Are you a real Native American Indian?"

Jason had taken out his pocketknife and was carving on a branch. "Yep," he said. "From the Ute tribe, around Cripple Creek Canyon."

"My dad read something in the newspaper last year about the reservation in Cripple Creek," recalled Isabel. "He said an elderly woman died during the winter because she didn't have heat. Is that true?"

Jason's eyes grew intense. He thrust his knife at the tree trunk. "That was my grandmother."

Isabel didn't know what to say. She pulled her knees to her chest and rested her head on them. "I'm sorry," she managed to get out.

"It's okay." His brown eyes looked sad. "She's with the Great Spirit now. I live with my grandmother's friend Maya. I'm *her* grandson now."

"Maya," said Isabel, sighing. "I've heard that name a lot lately."

"Hel-lo!" called a loud voice. "Isabel Morningsky, are you there?" It was Miss Kittle and a troop of girls come to rescue her.

"I better go," said Isabel. "My friends are probably worried about me." She climbed down a couple of branches and poked her head out. "I'm here, Miss Kittle." She waved then looked back to say goodbye to her new friend.

Jason gazed at her with a friendly smile. "I hope our paths cross again, Isabel Morningsky," he said.

Isabel turned to climb down another branch. "I hope our paths cross again too," she said. She peered up through the branches, but Jason Twofeathers was gone.

Chapter Nine
Pow Wow

Isabel lay across her bed with her headphones on, listening to music and writing in her clue book. It had been two weeks since she'd returned home from camp, but it seemed like only yesterday. She reviewed the last entry with a smile:

June 3, Met Jason Twofeathers at camp. He's from Ute Tribe. Woman he lives with named Maya – but she is older. Great frog catcher. ☺

Isabel flipped over on her back and stared at the ceiling. So many things seemed to be changing. New feelings flooded over her. She actually *liked* making jewelry at camp. And what was up with Jason Twofeathers? There was something mysterious yet so likeable about him. Maybe girl camp wasn't so bad after all. *I guess Dad knew best, after all,* she thought with a giggle. *I'm glad I went.*

Isabel rolled over onto her side and propped her head up on the pillow. This might be her last summer in Misty Springs for a long time. How could she leave her family? How could she leave Starlight? The warm feeling went away and she choked up.

"Somehow, Lord, make me willing to go to Boston and save the ranch."

"Hey, princess," said Dad, knocking on her door.

Isabel sat up. "Hey, Dad, come on in."

"I picked up a flyer from town today about a Pow Wow in Cripple Creek."

"Where's that?" Isabel asked. She brushed her hair out of her eyes and waited for her father's answer.

"It's a little town 150 miles north."

"What's a Pow Wow?"

Dad joined her on the bed. "It's a festival where Native Americans celebrate their heritage. They cook traditional food, perform traditional dances, and dress in traditional clothing called regalia."

Isabel remembered the museum. "You mean with all the cool feathers and things?"

"Yep. They sell lots of things made on the reservations too, and they have horse competitions. I thought it would be fun to take the horses and enter. Maybe Holly would like to come too."

Isabel bounced on the bed, grinning. "Dad, you're kidding! The kid I met at camp, the one I told you about, lives on the Cripple Creek reservation."

Dad had a twinkle in his eye. "So, what do you think?"

Isabel threw her arms around Dad's neck. "Yes! Double yes! When is it?"

"A week from tomorrow."

Isabel reached for her cell phone. "Please Dad, I have to text Holly right now!"

The week flew by as Isabel and Holly conjured up all kinds of ideas about Jason Twofeathers and the clay pot. Maybe Jason was the descendent of Sitting Bull, or perhaps Sacajawea was his great-great-grandmother. Could the mysterious Maya be his cousin or twin sister?

Isabel was so excited about the Pow Wow that she was sure she'd never be able to fall asleep the night before. But to her surprise, she woke up early that morning. An overwhelming sense of happiness flooded over her. "I think I better take the Clue Book today," she mused out loud. "I have a funny feeling that I'm going to need it."

Isabel heard the kitchen door slam. Holly's voice trailed up the stairs. "Good morning Mr. M., Mrs. M. Thanks a lot for inviting me."

Isabel dressed quickly and bounded down the stairs to greet her friend. "Hey, Holly!"

"I brought my trusty camcorder," she said patting it in her bag. "I've never been to a Pow Wow before. You never know when there'll be something interesting to shoot for a movie."

"That's right," agreed Isabel. "We could become famous."

It wasn't long before the Morningstars and Holly were tucked inside the blue pickup truck and headed for the Pow Wow.

Holly was glowing with excitement. "I think today's the day when I make my epic movie, Izzy."

Isabel didn't know why but she had this funny feeling that Holly might be right.

The time flew by as they drove to the Pow Wow Before they knew it, they were driving into the town. Mom was reading from a brochure. "Oh, this is interesting. Cripple Creek was nicknamed for the prospectors who came during the gold rush of the 1890s. Can you imagine? They found over two million ounces of gold."

Isabel looked at and Holly and smiled. She needed money. A lot of it. *I wonder if you can still pan for gold,* she pondered.

Holly read a sign aloud: "Pan for gold at Buzzard Gulch. You could be the next millionaire."

"Please, Mom," urged Isabel. "Can we stop?"

Dad looked at his watch and shook his head no.

"We don't have time, girls," answered Mom. "Maybe afterwards."

Isabel's heart sank. *This could have been my chance to find gold and save the ranch! And it just slipped through my fingers.* Isabel laid her head back on the seat and sighed.

Dad turned the truck into the county fairgrounds. A big banner was strung over the gate. It said: **Forty-Fifth Annual Cripple Creek Pow Wow**.

Holly had her camcorder out and was filming. "I don't think I've seen so many Native Americans in one place before."

"They're everywhere!" exclaimed Isabel.

A large group of dark-haired girls strolled by, laughing and talking.

"I love all the buckskin and colorful feather headdresses," said Mom.

"Oh, listen, it's so cute!" cooed Holly. "The girls' dresses jingle when they walk."

Holly and Isabel turned and looked at each other, beaming.

"Let's park the trailer over there, Dad," said Isabel, "next to that awesome Mustang."

Dad pulled the trailer around as Starlight and Patches whinnied loud enough for Isabel to hear.

"I think he likes the Mustang," said Isabel, smiling.

Dozens of trailers were parked in a row with horses grazing next to them. There were lawn chairs and coolers set out. It looked like a campsite.

Dad opened the door of the truck. "You girls take Starlight and Patches out and give them some feed and water. Then saddle them up and take them for a trot on the paths over there." Dad pointed. "We'll meet back here by 11:30 for the competition."

Dad leaned over and kissed Mom. "I'll be back soon." He put on his cowboy hat, winked at Mom, and disappeared into the crowd.

"Look, Izzy! Teepees, just like the ones we saw at the museum," admired Holly.

"I love the deer and moons on them," said Isabel. Her mouth began to water when she smelled the food drifting over from the food stands. "Holly, I don't think I can wait. Let's go get something to eat while the horses are grazing. Can we, Mom?"

"Go ahead, but be right back. We have lots to do before the competition."

"We will," the girls answered together. Isabel grabbed Holly's hand and pulled her down the gravel road towards the irresistible aromas.

Isabel and Holly stopped in front of a stand with a yellow striped tent. "Indian frybread," read Holly. "Honey butter, powdered sugar, or Indian taco."

"Powdered sugar for me," said Isabel to the woman behind the counter.

"Me too," said Holly.

"Mmmm, this is amazing," said Isabel with her mouth full of hot buttery bread and sugar.

The girls munched their frybread as they headed to a large, grassy area, where dozens of booths spread out, with Native Americans selling things.

Isabel and Holly stopped at a stand with a buffalo on top to look at the blankets and jewelry. "They're beautiful," said Holly, caressing them.

"Thank you," said a woman with big brown eyes.

Isabel took a big bite of her frybread. "Oh, look over there—pottery!" she said chewing. "Let's stop and look." Isabel squinted. "Holly, see that woman sitting in the rocking chair weaving that basket? She looks so familiar." Isabel felt a strange excitement come over her.

"Is that you, Isabel?" inquired the woman, looking up.

Isabel sprinted over. "Ms. Tabitha! It's so good to see you."

"Too long, child," said the old woman.

Isabel felt like a balloon ready to burst. "I found a picture of you in our attic. And Holly and I found an old clay pot with a poem on it. We took it to the museum."

"Slow down, child," said Tabitha with a laugh. "You're talking so fast."

A middle-aged woman with a turquoise beaded necklace walked up. "Maya, we need some change."

Isabel felt chills run down her spine. She stared at Ms. Tabitha. "I thought your name was Tabitha, but she just called you 'Maya.'"

"Maya is my middle name, given to me by my mother many moons ago."

Isabel's eyes widened. "Do you live in Cripple Creek? Do you know a boy named Jason Twofeathers?"

Tabitha set the basket down. "How do you know Jason?"

"I met him at Camp Tialocka this summer."

"So, you are the white dove he told me about." She smiled. "The boy lives with me. He is like my own son."

Isabel felt dizzy and put her hand on her head. Too many things were happening.

Holly walked up. "Izzy, what's going on?"

A young woman with a blue headband and feathers approached. "Is this your great-granddaughter, the one you talk so often about, Maya? The one that's named after you?"

Isabel stared at Tabitha. "Named after *you*? I'm Maya?"

"Child, I . . ." Tabitha stood up and reached out to her.

"I . . .I . . ." Isabel backed up and stumbled. "I have to get out here." She turned and hurried away down the path. Her heart exploded like a volcano that had been rumbling for ages. She couldn't stop the hot tears from streaming down her face. *Why didn't my parents tell me? Am I adopted? Are they ashamed of me?* She picked up a clod of dirt in the road and threw it at a tree.

Dad was walking back to the trailer whistling. He caught her gaze as she walked towards him. Isabel's eyes were red and swollen. "Izzy, what's the matter?"

Isabel sped past her dad, dodging him, and untied Starlight. "Why didn't you tell me?" she shouted. "Am I Native American? Am I even your daughter?" She grabbed Starlight's mane and jumped on his back. She gave him a fierce kick. "Get up!" Like the wind, Starlight took off and flew down the path.

"Isabel! Wait!" shouted Dad. He jumped on Patches and rode swiftly behind her.

Isabel plunged straight for the fence, and Starlight charged over it. *This can't be happening. It's all mixed up, I have to get away!*

Dad and Patches rode straight towards the fence and jumped over it too. "Izzy, stop!" Dad called behind her.

"Don't follow me, Daddy," Isabel choked out. She wiped her drippy nose on her sleeve. "Hee-yah!" She kicked Starlight again.

"Trust me! *I love you!*" he called out.

Isabel felt his words like a giant hand wrapping around her. "Whoa." She slowed Starlight down.

Dad rode up beside her. "Isabel. "

Even though Isabel felt angry and confused, she knew her dad loved her. She couldn't hold back this torrent of emotion any longer. She slumped over in the saddle, put her hands over her eyes, and sobbed.

"Come on, honey," said Dad. He dismounted Patches then reached up and gently pulled Isabel into his arms. He cradled her until her sobs slowed down. "Let me tell you a story."

They walked arm in arm over to shade of the aspen tree. "Sit down," he said, motioning with his hand.

Isabel sat, sniffling.

"It all started when I met your mom at a dance in Cripple Creek Parkway." Dad looked up thoughtfully and grinned. "Boy, could she dance! We felt like kindred spirits right from the start. We did everything together."

Isabel wiped her eyes on her sleeve, and a tiny smile curved her lips.

"My mother was a Ute Indian and my dad was British American. It came time to meet your mom's family, and right from the start Grandmother

Biltmore didn't like me. She had heard bad stories about Native Americans and didn't think I was good enough for her daughter. Your mom begged Grandmother Biltmore, but she had other plans for your mom's future. She wanted her to meet a rich man from Boston, have lots of grandchildren, and live near her."

Isabel sniffed. "Sounds like Gran."

"But my heart was here in Colorado. My family is here, and my heart belongs to the land."

Isabel was starting to understand why she loved nature so much. She had read about Natives Americans in school, how they respected the earth. Nothing brought her more joy than romping through the woods on Starlight or hearing a bubbling brook sing.

"Grandmother Biltmore realized that your mother and I were in love and finally agreed to let us get married on one condition: that we never raise our children according to Native American ways; that we kept it a secret." Dad hung his head. "She was ashamed."

Anger rose up in Isabel. "Didn't God make us all?"

Dad nodded in agreement. "Yes, He did. It was a hard decision, but we were madly in love and thought for sure that, in time, Gran's heart would soften."

Isabel pulled her knees to her chest and rested her chin on them. How could she not have known this for eleven years?

"So, we were married. Two years later you were born. You had the cutest head of dark black hair and beautiful rose lips."

Isabel smiled.

"It was early in the dawn," Dad began to recite,

> "A dove came to call,
> Sweetly singing in my tent;
> With hair the color of night.
> The sun laughed, the deer leapt,
> My spirit sang for joy, my sweet Maya."

Isabel gasped. "Daddy, *you* wrote that?"

Dad turned red and nodded. "I was so happy when you were born. My spirit soared. And I still am. Gran wanted you to have a Christian name, so we named you Isabel and put Maya in the middle." He drew a deep, sorrowful breath. "I'm sorry we didn't tell you. Can you forgive your mother and me?"

Isabel rushed into her dad's arms and hugged him tight. A tear trickled down her cheek and she nodded. She pulled back and gazed into her dad's eyes. "What about Gran and the ranch?"

"When you were born, she offered us a lot of money to buy the ranch, so we could raise you in comfort. But she thinks I have secretly been teaching you Native American ways because of the horses. She wants to take back the loan unless you live with her and go to school in Boston." Dad cleared his throat. "I think I met a man today who wants to buy the ranch. We could use the profit to buy a nice little home in town and pay Grandmother Biltmore back." The light went out of his eyes and he looked down.

Isabel couldn't believe her ears. "And give up the horses? Give up the land? No! I'm going to that school, Dad. Winners never quit and quitters never win!" Isabel choked up. "For I serve the mighty God that lives deep within!" she finished. "You love the ranch."

"But I love you more." Dad shook his head. "I've kept this secret for so long and I've never felt good about it. His forehead wrinkled and his lips twisted like he was in pain. "There were times I felt it eating away at my insides. But now" — a tear ran down his cheek — "it's as if a cage door has been open and I feel so relieved." His voice cracked.

"Daddy." Isabel put her hands on her dad's cheeks and caressed his face.

"We tried to do things in our own strength, but I can see that God's ways are best," said Dad. "There's a verse in the Bible, 'You shall know the truth and it shall set you free.' That has clearly come true today."

Dad looked into Isabel's eyes and stroked her cheek. "Isabel, I love you."

It was as if a huge dam broke that had been held back for eleven years. They fell into each other's arms and sobbed like babies.

Chapter Ten
Dresses with Bells

The news spread like wildfire in the Native American community that Tabitha's long-lost great-granddaughter was at the Pow Wow. All of Tabitha's friends and neighbors wanted to stop by and take a look.

As Isabel brushed down Starlight, a group of Native American girls dressed in red-and-blue buckskin dresses approached her.

"Are you Maya's granddaughter?" asked one of the girls.

Isabel swallowed hard. "Yeah, I guess I am."

"We think you should be a part of our dance," said another girl.

"I . . . I don't know. I've never done that before."

"We can teach you. It's easy as pie," said an eight-year-old girl with a red zigzag headband. "I'm Katie," she said, smiling. "But you can call me Spotted Fawn."

Something welled up from deep inside of Isabel. A peace, a joy, a knowing that this was where she belonged.

Isabel nodded vigorously and smiled. "Yes!" What new adventures lay ahead she didn't know, but what she did know was that she wanted to do this with all her heart.

The girls whisked her away to the costume tent to give her a special outfit called regalia. Once inside, they gave her a beautiful, tan buckskin dress with turquoise beading. *My favorite color!* The fringe on the bottom held little bells that jingled as she walked. *That's the sound we heard when we drove up,* thought Isabel. The sound tickled the back of her neck. She felt aglow inside with happiness.

The girls gathered around her like a gaggle of geese, braiding her hair and giving her feathers to wear in her headband.

One girl stepped closer. "We have decided to give you a Native American name," she announced. "We all voted. It's Mourning Dove." Isabel smiled.

She loved the peaceful *coo* that mourning doves made.

"Thank you," she said, beaming. For the first time in her life she felt shy. She reached down and ran her hand along the dress. It was so soft and pretty. It smelled like the outdoors that she loved so much. *I was made to wear this dress.*

"Time to practice," said Mrs. Silverfox, entering the room and clapping her hands. The girls gathered together around her. After giving ten minutes of instructions, she turned on the music. The girls began to swing their arms and tap their feet to the beat.

"Oops, sorry," said Isabel, bumping into tall girl with glasses. Then she backed up and stepped on Spotted Fawn's foot.

"Ouch!"

"Sorry, I'm so clumsy." *I'm never going to get this!*

Mrs. Silverfox held up her arms. "Wait, stop the music. I think some of you are thinking too hard. I want you to picture yourself as a great bald eagle soaring into the wind. This *is* the Eagle Dance, after all. Don't think about it too much. *Feel* the music. Okay, let's try it again."

Isabel closed her eyes when the music began. She felt the wind blowing in her hair as she soared towards the sun in the blue sky. She heard the beat and felt it in her feet. It was easier to follow now. *I'm doing it. And it's so fun!*

Laughter and joking filled the next hour as Isabel became an Indian princess dancing with the group. Everyone was so nice. It wasn't long before Isabel felt right at home.

"You catch on very fast," said Spotted Fawn.

Isabel couldn't believe she loved to dance this much. She even liked wearing the buckskin dress. "Holly's never going to believe this." She chuckled to herself.

A tall, Native American woman with dark, braided hair and a clipboard peeked inside the tent. "We're ready for you, girls."

Giggling girls scurried for feathers and last-minute peeks in the mirror. Then they filed out one by one and sauntered over to the Pow Wow ring, where they stood in an eagle formation. The drum began its steady beat as the girls tapped their feet and swung their arms.

The crowd stood and cheered. Isabel's spirit soared. She smiled at the jingling sound that the girls' dresses made.

When the last drumbeat ended, Mom and Dad rushed up to Isabel. She jumped into her dad's arms. "Did you guys see me?"

"I couldn't have missed the prettiest girl out there," said Dad, squeezing her tight.

Mom leaned in and kissed her. "Honey, you were amazing. A real natural."

"Isabel Morningsky?" said a voice from behind her. She turned around. Jason Twofeathers stood there with a huge grin on his face.

"Yep," she said, sheepishly shrugging her shoulders. "It's me."

"That was really awesome. You didn't tell me you were a Native American."

"I didn't know . . . until today."

Jason looked puzzled.

When the other girls saw Isabel talking to Jason, they ran over. "She's our honorary Indian maiden," one said. "She's Tabitha's great-granddaughter."

Jason folded his arms, and his eyebrows shot up. "The one she always talks about?"

"Yep," said Spotted Fawn. "We gave her a Native American name too. It's Mourning Dove."

Jason looked at Isabel and smiled. "Good name."

Tabitha slowly hobbled out, leaning on a cane.

"Grandmother," Jason offered, "lean on me."

She put her hand on Jason's shoulder and stood in front of Isabel. "You have made me so proud, great-granddaughter." She held out her hand. "This is my gift." She encircled Isabel's neck with a beautiful silver and turquoise necklace.

The girls in the group gasped.

"This was *my* great-grandmother's," Tabitha told Isabel. "Princess Maya Leaping Deer Morningsky, of the Ute tribe that lived in the shadow of the Red Mountain."

Isabel was speechless again. Dad picked her up and swung her around. "I always said you were a princess."

Isabel kept her regalia on for the rest of the day. She even wore it when she rode Starlight in the competitions.

Jason Twofeathers rode up to her after the bareback race. "Nice race," he said with a twinkle in his eye. "Sorry I had to win."

"That's okay," replied Isabel. "Second place isn't so bad coming in next to you. You and Thunder are a great team."

Jason dismounted. "I have something for you." He reached into his saddle bag and pulled out a bundle of hawk feathers. "This is to weave into Starlight's mane. I'll show you how."

Isabel caught her breath. "How beautiful! Thank you, Jason." She felt like part of the family now. Jason and she braided Starlight's tail and put the feathers in it. "There," she said, smiling. "Now you are a proper Native American horse."

Mr. Whitehorse, the Grand Marshall of the Pow Wow, rode up to her dressed in a full chief's headdress. "Miss Isabel Morningsky?"

She jogged over to his horse. "Yes?"

"Your wonderful story has reached my ears. You are quite a good rider. We would be honored if you would ride with us in the parade at the end of the Pow Wow today."

Isabel couldn't believe her ears. She whirled. "Can I, Mom?"

"Of course, sweetie," Mom replied. "Mr. Whitehorse, we would be honored."

A warm, summer breeze blew through Isabel's hair that night as she rode Starlight in the parade under the silvery, moonlit sky. A rainbow of fireworks twinkled in the heavens above her. "Oohs and ahs" filled the stadium.

Isabel stroked Starlight's neck. "Look, boy. Isn't it beautiful?" A lovely feeling flowed all around her. At that moment she felt as if everything was perfect. She glanced at the crowds of people watching them and saw that Holly stood near the road, video taping.

Holly waved. "It will be the greatest movie ever!"

Isabel smiled and waved back. She glanced over the crowd and spied her dad. "Who's that man with the dark moustache talking with Dad?" she muttered. Then she sucked in her breath in remembrance. "Oh no! He's the man who wants to buy our ranch." Her heart sank. She *had* to go to Boston and save the ranch. That man reminded Isabel that there was no other way now.

"Quitters never win," she murmured to herself. She felt a heavy weight in her chest. She had just found her new, Native American family and loved them so much. She didn't want to leave them now. "Please Lord," Isabel prayed silently, "I need a miracle."

When the Pow Wow ended, everyone packed up to leave. Isabel hugged her great-grandmother goodbye melting into her arms. Tabitha was soft and warm and the smell of buckskin clung to her like a sweet perfume. "I don't want to go," she said to Tabitha, squeezing her. "I wish you lived with us."

Tabitha held her face with her tan, weathered hands. Her eyes shone; a tear slipped down her cheek. "It won't seem like we are so far apart if we write to each other." She handed a piece of paper to Isabel with handwriting scribbled on it. "Here is my address." It was a program from the Pow Wow. It said, "To my beloved Mourning Dove, you are forever in my heart. Write me often. I will eagerly wait to hear from you. Love, Great-grandmother Tabitha."

Chapter Eleven
The Letter

July turned hot. The sky shone a brilliant blue as Isabel skipped to the mailbox. She was hoping to get a letter from Great-grandmother Tabitha. It had only been two weeks since the Pow Wow, but it seemed like a million years to Isabel.

She pulled out the bundle of mail and flipped through it. "Hmmm, saddles for sale at the Farm and Saddle shop. Maybe Dad and I can get one." She eyed a hand-written, light-blue envelope with no return address. *A letter from Tabitha!* She slipped it in her jeans pocket. "I'll save it to read up in the tree house."

Isabel dashed inside house and down to the kitchen, where Mom was making lunch. She eyed the mound of fresh cucumbers from the vegetable garden resting on the counter. "Mmmm! Can we have cucumber sandwiches for lunch?"

"That's a great idea," said Mom. She wiped her hands on her apron.

Isabel felt antsy and jiggled her foot. "Do you need any help?" she asked.

"Not right now, but you can come back and set the table in half an hour."

"Okay, be back soon. I have something I need to do in the tree house," she said over her shoulder. "Bye." In a flash, Isabel rushed out the door and slammed it behind her.

"I can't wait," she said, skipping across the yard. "I can't wait to hear what Tabitha has to say. Maybe she got the pattern for the deerskin dress we're going to make together."

Isabel hurried up the rope ladder that led to the top of the tree house. She plopped down on the brown chair, careful to avoid the spot where her fudgesicle melted last week, and tore open the letter.

My Dearest Isabel,

Please do the right thing and come live with me. Your father has worked so hard in building the ranch. It would be a shame if he would have to lose it. You can ride horses here in my private stables and meet a lot of fine young people your age. Answer me soon, for there are arrangements to be made.

Grandmother Biltmore

Isabel gasped. Gran's words pierced her heart like a sword. She knew she had to go, but how could she leave now when she just found out the secret? And her new great-grandmother would be visiting tomorrow. Isabel caught her breath. *I wonder if Gran knows I know the secret.*

Isabel paced back and forth in the tree house. *Think, Isabel, think! Should I tell Mom and Dad about the letter?* Gran's words echoed in her ears like a bad dream, "Do the right thing."

Isabel hung her head.

When Isabel didn't want mashed potatoes at dinner, Mom asked, "Are you feeling okay, dear?"

Isabel shrugged her shoulders, "Just tired is all."

When she passed up hot apple pie with ice cream, Dad said, "Izzy, are you sick?"

Isabel sighed and squirmed in her chair. A wave of nausea swept over her. It was as if Gran's words in the letter were trying to poison her.

"Nope, I'm okay," she said, trying to be brave. Here, let me have a bite." She poked her fork into the apple pie and pushed it around. "Can I be excused, please?"

Isabel trudged up to her room and threw herself on the bed. Tabitha would be visiting tomorrow, and Gran's letter spoiled everything. She punched the bed. *Why does she spoil everything?*

Isabel couldn't sleep that night. At midnight she climbed out of bed to get a drink of water. When she came back, the Bible lying on her nightstand caught her eye. She crawled into bed and opened it up, flipping to the verse her Sunday school class was studying: Philippians 4:6. She had underlined it: "Be anxious for nothing, but by prayer with thanksgiving let your requests be known to God, and the peace that passes understanding will guard your heart and mind in Christ Jesus."

She slipped to her knees. "How can I be thankful in all this?" She buried her head in her blankets. "I know. I can be thankful that I found out the secret. But everything seems so jumbled up. Lord, I'm not smart enough to figure this out on my own. I *need* You to guide me. If I have to go to Boston so my parents can keep the ranch, give me strength, show me a sign." She took a deep breath and let it out like that was the end of that.

A sweet peace enveloped Isabel as she climbed back in bed. She pulled the sheets up to her chin and drifted off to sleep.

The morning broke crisp and sunny. The scent of fresh-cut grass floated through Isabel's open window. Her new great-grandmother was coming today for a visit. Isabel felt giddy. What a change! How could she feel so happy today when she'd been so miserable yesterday?

She hopped out of bed and dashed downstairs. "Mom! *Mom!* I want to make something special for Great-grandmother today."

"I thought you might. Look at this cute idea I found on the Internet."

Isabel took the recipe out of Mom's hand and read it. "Ice-cream-cone teepees." She wrinkled her brow. "You don't have to cook anything, do you?"

Mom's eyes twinkled. "Nope, that's the best part."

Isabel's face lit up. She was relieved. Things didn't turn out so well when she cooked. "I love it, Mom." She hugged her. "Thank you."

Mom gave her a kiss. "I love you too, Isabel."

Isabel ran to the cabinets and opened them wide. "Do we have all the stuff for it?"

"I think so."

As Isabel got out the ingredients she whistled. "What should we do first when Grandmother Tabitha comes?"

"Why don't we have snacks," said Mom, "and then sit out in the gazebo. It's such a nice day."

Isabel liked that idea.

The time flew by as Isabel and Mom assembled the teepees. First, Isabel cut the cones in half. Then she slathered peanut butter on the top and stuck pretzel sticks out through the "roof."

"Now comes the fun part," said Isabel, "dipping them in chocolate." Isabel stepped back to look at the tray of teepees. She put her finger up to her chin. Something was missing. "I know what they need."

Isabel scampered over to the cupboard and found Mom's birthday frosting tubes. Carefully, Isabel drew moons and deer on the teepees. "There," she said, approving. "Just like the ones we saw at the Pow Wow."

"She's going to love them, Isabel," said Mom. She looked up at the clock. "Looks like we finished just in time."

Isabel raced to her room to put on the necklace Grandmother Tabitha had given her at the Pow Wow. She tied it around her neck and gazed in the mirror. *"Am I an Indian princess?"* She held the necklace near her heart, closed her eyes, and sighed. At last she had a grandma who loved her for just being herself. No strings attached.

Isabel heard the rumbling of a truck driving up the road and darted to the window to see. It was Grandmother Tabitha! She quickly finished dressing and rushed outside to greet her.

Tabitha wore a bright-orange, flowered top. Her long, black hair was tied in a braid and she held a blue and yellow, woven basket in her hand. She opened her arms when she saw Isabel.

"Great-grandmother!" cried Isabel, rushing into her arms.

"It's good to see you, child." Tabitha drew her close and stroked her hair.

"Mmmm. I love you. I'm so glad you're here."

"I have something for you," said the old woman. She held out the basket to Isabel.

"This is for me?"

"Yes, you can keep your treasures in it." The woman's dark eyes glowed.

"I love it. Thank you so much."

Isabel took Tabitha by the hand and pulled her across the lawn. She could hardly wait to show her what they made. "I have something for you too."

Tabitha was slow. She hobbled while she leaned on Isabel. "Careful up the stairs, Great-grandmother." Isabel didn't want anything to happen to this dear, sweet woman. "How old are you, anyway?"

"Ninety-two on my last birthday. The Great Spirit has been good to me."

Isabel felt warm inside as she held Tabitha's hand.

Mom rushed up to the porch. "Tabitha, it's good to see you. It's so nice not to have to hide any more secrets. Come into the kitchen."

Tabitha nodded and smiled.

Isabel led Tabitha to the counter, where the teepees sat on a sliver try. "Look, Great-grandmother," said Isabel proudly. "I made them for you."

"Your teepees look good enough to eat," Tabitha chuckled.

"They are!"

Tabitha shuffled over to the table and sat down.

"Can I pour you some iced tea?" asked Mom.

Tabitha nodded and helped herself to a teepee. She set it on the plate in front of her.

"Let's bite ours at the same time," Isabel said, smiling. "One, two, three . . ."

Crunch! The two of them bit down together.

"Mmmm, delicious! You are a good cook, Isabel Maya," said Tabitha.

Isabel blushed. She wanted to say something but her mouth was full of sweet, chocolaty peanut butter and pretzels. She swallowed. "Thank you! No one had ever said that before."

Isabel showed Grandmother Tabitha the story she wrote about Native Americans for school and read it aloud. They were crunching on their third teepees when the back door opened and Dad stepped in from chores.

"Grandmother Tabitha," he said tenderly. He bent down and kissed her cheek. "It's like a holiday having you come to visit."

She smiled, looked into his eyes, and caressed his cheek with her wrinkled, brown hand. "I'm proud of you, Grandson, for bringing such a miracle to light." She looked over at Isabel beaming.

"I thank God He gave us the courage to do it," agreed Dad.

The old woman stood. "Did you get what I asked you to get for Isabel?"

"I'll be right back. I left it in the barn." Dad vanished out the back door.

"It's such a beautiful day. Let's go outside and sit in the gazebo," said Mom.

Tabitha nodded.

"I'll help you, Great-grandmother. " Isabel held out her arm.

The three of them sat in the shade of the gazebo that was dressed in pink roses. Purple petunias hung in baskets all around, and the smell of lavender mingled with roses perfumed the air.

Isabel dived into the hammock and swung back and forth. "This is the best day ever."

Dad walked across the yard wearing his blue jeans and cowboy hat. He was carrying a zigzag woven blanket.

"What's this?" Isabel asked, jumping down.

"It's a story blanket," said Dad. "The one Tabitha made when you were born."

Isabel touched the soft blanket with the red and brown zigzag design. "I don't remember it."

"That's because you never got it," said Mom. "We hid it because of Grandmother Biltmore."

Grandmother Tabitha looked sad. She nodded to Dad and he held it out to Isabel. "Here, it's yours now to keep. If you unroll it, you can lie on it and listen to Tabitha tell stories."

"Native American stories?" Isabel was all a flutter inside. "Right now?"

"Yep," answered Dad.

Isabel knelt down and carefully unrolled the blanket. Beautiful bluebirds were sewn in the middle of it. She loved bluebirds. She sat down on the blanket and wiggled around until she felt comfortable. She finally tucked her hands behind her head. "Okay, I'm ready."

Tabitha cleared her throat and leaned forward, towards Isabel. "Many moons ago, there was a young eagle named Ben Sawee. He was brave and strong. He was out hunting for a nice, juicy mouse or a fish to bring home to his family for dinner. The winds began to blow hard and swirl in a circle. Dark clouds enveloped him like a cloak.

Ben Sawee knew he must not run, but he must face the storm. So he looked up and flew higher into the strong breeze that beat against his chest. His eyes stung, but he kept climbing higher into the wind. His wings were tired. Lightning flashed. 'Be brave Ben Sawee!' he heard a voice say, 'the storm will lift you higher.'

"With that, a great torrent of air scooped him up and lifted him above the storm clouds. The sun above smiled down on him. The thunder crashed and the rains poured down below him, but Ben Sawee was safe and warm above the mighty gale. Ben Sawee learned to trust his Creator."

Isabel sat up, wide eyed. She felt like she had been given the answer to her prayer: *Trust*. "I'll be right back," she said. She dashed over to the tree house and hid behind it. Her heart hammered in her chest. She pulled out Grandmother Biltmore's terrible letter and tore it to pieces.

It was as if a huge hand had picked her up and set her above the storm clouds. She fell to her knees and cried. "Thank you, God. I can breathe again!"

Chapter Twelve
The Reporter

The rest July flew by, and soon August came with scorching heat. The corn in Isabel's garden began to wilt, and the pond was drying up.

As Isabel walked down the stairs for breakfast one sweltering morning, she heard her parents talking in the kitchen.

"What's this?" asked Dad, flipping through the mail.

"Grandmother Biltmore's letter," Mom answered in a low voice. "With instructions for preparation and school registration."

Isabel stopped at the door and listened. She didn't know what to do. She didn't want to go to

Gran's crummy old school. Was she being selfish? It didn't feel like there was a solution to her problem anywhere that she could see. She would have to try and trust in God's solution, which she couldn't see.

Dad pounded his fist on the table. "The nerve of that woman! We have to sell the ranch, Grace. I've made my decision. The man is coming over today to look at it. It's the only way to keep Isabel with us."

"I can be happy living anywhere, Sam, as long as you and Isabel are with me. I just feel so sad about losing the horses. It was your dream. What will we do with Starlight? It will crush Isabel to have to sell him."

"I thought about that," said Dad. "Maybe Holly could keep him, so Izzy could visit him.

A dark cloud hung over Isabel when she and Holly rode off to Dinosaur Creek later that day. Isabel felt the comforting sway of Starlight's gait and gazed at the aspen-covered hills as if it were the last time she would see these old friends. A mourning dove flew by and cooed for its mate.

"They always sound so sad, cooing like that," said Holly.

"I wish I was one of them today. I would fly away and hide," lamented Isabel.

"Poor Izzy," said Holly. "Do you want to race?"

Isabel knew Holly was only trying to cheer her up. "Nah," she said, "I don't feel like racing today."

"Izzy, you don't have to go. Stay here and let your dad sell the ranch. At least you would all be together."

"We can't lose the ranch, Holly. My dad loves this place. I love this place. It's all I've ever known. I know he said he loved me more, but I feel like I would be letting him down if I don't go. And what about Starlight and the rest of the horses? We can't just sell them all."

When they reached the creek, they dug up a couple of rocks and caught a bullfrog, but Isabel let it go. "I'm sorry. I'm no fun today. Let's go back."

When Isabel and Holly rode back from the creek, they saw the man with the dark mustache who wanted to buy the ranch. He drove off in a white Bronco. A pain rose in Isabel's chest.

Mom waved at Isabel from the porch. She seemed excited about something and ran out to meet them. "A newspaper reporter from Denver called today. He wants to come out and interview you."

"What for?" asked Isabel as she tied up Starlight.

"It seems that the Native American Society of Cripple Creek Canyon heard how you found out about your heritage at the Pow Wow. Good publicity for them, I guess."

"Wow," said Holly. "You'll be famous!"

"I wonder how they found out," said Isabel.

Holly stepped forward and bowed. "Holly Haddelburg, worldwide movie producer, at your service."

"Holly, you're the best friend anyone could ever have," vowed Isabel.

Holly's face glowed. "That's my job."

"What did you tell the reporter?" Isabel asked Mom.

"I said I'll ask my daughter."

"Mom, I really want to do the interview," Isabel said as they walked across the lawn, "but on one condition."

Mom gave Isabel a puzzled look.

"That the newspaper also reports about the poor living conditions on the reservation. Someone has to do something about it."

They walked up the front porch steps together. A large package rested by the front door, addressed to Isabel.

Isabel bent down and picked it up. "What's this?"

"It's from Gran. It's . . . your uniforms for school. She wants you to try them on. Isabel, I don't want you to go," said Mom. "We'll find a way to stay together."

Holly looked like she was going to cry.

"I have to do it, Mom, for Daddy."

On Saturday, Cole Moody from the *Denver Chronicle* came over, flashing his camera and his big, white smile. He was a young man of twenty-five, with a warm personality and sandy blonde hair. He was neatly dressed in khaki pants and a blue polo shirt with a lanyard around his neck that said *Denver Chronicle*.

"Hey, squirt," he said to Isabel. "I guess you have a cool story to tell."

Isabel felt very serious as she sat down with Cole and told him about how she almost put the clues together and how she and Holly found the clay pot.

"It was like God was unfolding the secret to me all along, but I didn't want to believe it." Isabel looked down. "It wasn't until we went to the Pow Wow that the whole thing tumbled out."

Isabel went on for two hours and told how her Grandmother Biltmore was embarrassed that Isabel was Native American and how she'd tried to hide it from her since she was born. She explained how her family would lose the ranch if Isabel didn't go to Boston with her grandmother. She talked about Jason Twofeather's grandmother too, and how she died because she had no heat.

When they had eaten the last cookie and gulped down the last glass of lemonade, Cole stood up. "Thank you, young lady," he said with a smile and shook Isabel's hand. "It was a real pleasure meeting you."

"You're welcome," said Isabel. "Are you really going to print my story in the newspaper?"

Cole's eyes twinkled. "You bet I am."

Isabel sat on the porch swing and watched Cole walk over to his car. She remembered the picture on the wall, with the Bible verse on it, which she and Holly had looked at the day the blizzard hit. "I will cover you with my wings, until the storm passes by." As Isabel stood up to wave goodbye, an overwhelming sense of peace flooded over her.

A week later after breakfast, Dad picked up the *Denver Chronicle* from the mailbox.

"Hurry, Daddy! Get to the special feature section," urged Isabel.

"Well, what do you know," said Dad, grinning. He opened it up and spread the newspaper across the kitchen table. "Isabel's on the first page. There's even a big picture of her in her regalia at the Pow Wow with Tabitha."

Mom stopped washing dishes and sat down next to Isabel. She wrapped an arm around her. "You looked so cute in your outfit that day, honey."

"It was one of the best days of my life," Isabel sighed.

Mom looked at Dad. "Mother Biltmore called while you were gone. She wants to talk with you about making arrangements to take Isabel to the airport. She said she would call back later."

"That woman sure knows how to test one's faith," growled Dad.

Isabel didn't want to think about it. She didn't want to go. But her love for her dad and the ranch compelled her on. "Dad, it will be okay," said Isabel, trying to convince herself.

The phone rang in the den. Mom raised her eyebrows and glanced over at Dad. "It's probably for you."

Dad stormed into the den and picked up the phone.

Isabel ran after him and stood by the desk. "Hello!" Dad barked. "Oh, oh, I'm so sorry. I thought you were someone else." He wiped the sweat from his hand on his white t-shirt and listened intently for several minutes.

Isabel jiggled her foot and leaned over to Dad. "What is it? What's going on?"

Dad covered the phone. "Wait a minute, honey."He put his hand on his head. "Is this for real? Let me call my wife . . . Grace!"

Mom rushed into the den. "What is it? Is everything all right?"

Isabel looked at her Dad quizzically, "Daddy?"

"The Native American Historical Society read the column in the newspaper. They also received a very impressive video documenting what happened that day."

Holly! thought Isabel.

"They have a government grant to preserve Native American culture. They want to lend us the money for the ranch."

Mom put her hand over her heart, "It's a miracle!"

"Their one condition is that we allow their horse trainers to come to Angel Ridge Ranch and teach a class once a month to educate the public on Native American horsemanship. They also want Isabel to help them. It's good publicity."

Isabel beamed. "Yes!" she shouted, jumping up and down. "Double yes!"

Mom closed her eyes and pulled Isabel into her arms. She hugged her as tears streamed down her cheeks.

Dad went back to talking on the phone. "Thank you so much, Mrs. Whitehorse. You have no idea what this means to us. Goodbye."

Dad picked Isabel up and spun her around.

"They're sending over their delegate next week to work up the details." He gave her a big kiss. "Alleluia!"

"You don't have to go to Boston now," said Mom, sniffing. "I'll call Gran right away."

"Yippee!" cried Isabel. "We don't have to sell the ranch!"

Dad grabbed Mom's and Isabel's hands, and they all danced around the room. Then they plopped down on the couch, laughing. At the same moment, Dad and Isabel faced each other and stood up. "Winners never quit," they chanted, "and quitters never win, for we serve the mighty God, that lives deep within!"

"Woo hoo!" shouted Isabel.

"You two!" Mom said, laughing and crying at the same time. "You two are the best family anyone could ever have."

"The real glory goes to God, Mom. We could have never done it without Him." Isabel looked at Dad. "It's like that verse that you shared with me came true. What was it again?"

Dad smiled. "You're right, Izzy. John 8:32, 'You shall know the truth, and the truth shall set you free.'"

Isabel knew just what to do when the blizzard came because her parents talked about it beforehand. Her mother posted a list on an inside cupboard so they would always be prepared. Here is a list for you to share with your parents. You can make a list too and post it where every member in the family can find it.

Blizzard Safety

There are some ways you can plan before a disaster occurs. You may never have to use these tips, but you will want to know them just in case.

1. Come up with a family plan for disasters and post it where every family member knows where it is.
2. Make a blizzard and storm kit ahead of time and keep it where it can be found easily.
3. Include a battery-operated radio with extra batteries.

4. Have several flashlights with extra batteries-- avoid candles because of the fire hazard.
5. Have an emergency food supply of canned goods, can opener, and water.

6. Designate a spot in the hall closet to keep thermal underwear, hats, and socks.
7. Keep board games or arts and crafts for kids; it could last several days.
8. Children may be tempted to go outside but should not go — temperatures are cold enough for frostbite.
9. Eat for body heat.
10. Jump up and down in the house to stay warm, but do not overexert·

Sources

"Blizzards and Snow Storm Facts and Safety Guides," www.chiff.com/blizzard safety

"Dangerous Weather," www.edu/kids/dangerwx/blizzard, " Kids Crossing."

"Preparing for Winter Storms and Blizzards," www.MyGreatHome.com
www.RedCross.org

How to Make Christmas Card Place Mats

Every year Isabel saves all the Christmas cards they receive, puts them in a special flowered box, and saves them in her closet. You can start a tradition all your own by gathering your friends every year before Christmas and sharing your cards back and forth to make place mats. Of course, you should have lots of Holly's chocolaty confetti candy on hand to eat while you work.

Materials

- New or used Christmas cards
- A 12 x 18 inch piece of red, green or yellow construction paper for each place mat
- Glue stick
- Scissors
- 12 x 18 inch piece of Christmas wrapping paper for each place mat — red-and-green checks are great
- 5 x 7 inch colored paper or Christmas stationery
- When you are finished, an office supply or teacher store will laminate them for just a few dollars each.

Instructions

1. Measure and cut a piece of wrapping paper to fit on top of the construction paper. It should be about 11 x 17 inches. Using a glue stick, glue it on top of the construction paper, centering it.
2. Clip off the four corners of the construction paper (about 2 inches long). Cut the wrapping paper corners off, too.
3. Cut the picture and words from the cards that you want to use.
4. Arrange the cards around the edges of the construction paper where you like and glue them on. Leave a 5 x 7 inch space in the middle for the poem.

Take a 5 x 7 inch piece of colored paper or stationery and write a poem in your neatest writing and glue it in the middle. Use your five senses. For example:

1. Christmas *looks* like a bright star, leading three wise men on a wonderful journey.
2. Christmas *smells* like a freshly cut pine tree standing near the fireplace.
3. Christmas *tastes* like Grandma's sweet sugar cookies baking in the oven.

4. Christmas *sounds* like Holly singing in the play at church.

5. Christmas *feels* like the best day of the year!

Now you try! Fill in the blanks:

Christmas looks like_____

(where)_____

Christmas smells like_____

(where)_____

Christmas tastes like_____

(where)_____

Christmas sounds like_____

(where)_____

Christmas feels like _____

(where)_____

Holly's Famous Confetti Candy

Holly made up an easier microwave recipe for Isabel, so it wouldn't burn the next time. I think you will have a lot fun making and eating it!

1. Melt 2 bags of chocolate chips in the microwave. Start with 1-minute intervals and stir each time. It shouldn't take more than 2-3 times.
2. Line a 9 x 13 inch pan with wax or parchment paper.
3. Pour melted chocolate in the pan and spread it out evenly.
4. Press in your favorite shortbread cookies, tiny candy canes, miniature candy bars, nuts, peanut butter cups, M&M's, and pretzels. Shake candy sprinkles over the top when finished. Store in a cool place for 30 minutes or until firm.
5. Peel and break off pieces to put in tins or leave whole and let friends and family at a party, break off the piece they want.

For a different flavor, you could use white or mint chips instead of chocolate or sprinkle them over the top.

About the Author

Jan May has been teaching children to write for over twenty years. She is the author of *Creative Writing Made Easy-Introducing Isabel, Isabel's Closet,* and *Creative and Crafty Writing* — the fun way to get kids to write. She is a graduate of the Institute of Children's Literature and has a college background in Biblical Studies and Christian Education from North Central University in Minneapolis, Minnesota.

Upcoming New Millennium Girl books:

Isabel's Fun Fair Fiasco and *Cali's Contest of Courage,* coming soon. Sign up for our free newsletter and stay informed of the latest books, crafts and recipes for kids @ www.NewMillenniumGirlBooks.com

Calling all girls who love to write!

Look for the *New Millennium Girls Creative Writing Curriculum* and create a story all your own. A real princess moves in next door to Isabel. Design and color paper doll outfits for her and Isabel.